Amos Daragon

BOOK FOUR
THE CURSE OF FREYJA

www.amosdaragon.co.uk

First published in Canada by Les Intouchables MMIII

First published in Great Britain by Scribo MMX,
Scribo, a division of Book House, an imprint of
The Salariya Book Company
25 Marlborough Place, Brighton, BN1 1UB
www.salariya.com

Book Design by David Salariya

English edition © The Salariya Book Company
& Bailey Publishing Associates MMX

Printed and bound in Dubai

Cover Illustration by David Frankland

The text for this book is set in Cochin
The display types are set in CCNearMyth-Legends

AMOS DARAGON

BOOK FOUR

THE CURSE OF FREYJA

BRYAN PERRO

English Edition by
Glynne Yeardley

Scriba
A division of Book House

BRYAN PERRO

Bryan Perro was born in Shawinigan, Quebec, in 1968. He has trained as a drama teacher and actor, as well as obtaining a masters degree in Education. His best-selling series, *Amos Daragon*, has been translated into 19 languages and Book One, *The Mask Wearer*, has sold over one million copies in Quebec alone. Perro has been awarded a variety of prizes for his fiction, including the 2006 Quebec Youth Prize for Fiction and Fantasy.

Amos Daragon
The Curse of Freyja
Prologue

Nothing was right among the Nordic gods. Freyja, goddess of Fertility, had quarrelled with Odin and had spitefully placed a curse on his favourite creation, the Beorites. Her curse means that all Beorite offspring die in infancy so that the race faces extinction. The Beorites decide to sail to Freyja's island to try to reason with her. Amos Daragon, the mask-wearer, is desperate to continue his search for his mother who has been captured by goblins, but he agrees to go with them. Their journey will be strewn with dangers: a witch, sea serpents, a griffon and the Grey Man are just some of the creatures sent by the god Loki to make sure the young mask-wearer and his friends do not succeed. Fortunately our heroes will be helped by brave and faithful friends who, like Amos, are determined to put the world back into balance.

CHAPTER ONE

BABA YAGA

As she walked, the old woman muttered beneath her breath. She cursed just about everything; the gods, the singing of the birds and even the warmth of spring. She carried a bag of grain slung across her shoulder to feed the birds. She scattered it around her with great theatrical sweeps. Dozens of birds flew down from all directions to enjoy this unexpected feast. But this glorious spring day was to be their last: the grain was poisoned.

Baba Yaga had once been a radiantly beautiful young woman, married to a handsome young man and living in a lovely little village full of flowers and children's laughter. Her dearest wish had been to have children of her own, but after many years of marriage, the gods had not smiled upon her and she was still childless. She waited patiently for many long years but never became a mother.

One day a terrible storm hit the village and Baba Yaga's cottage was struck by lightning. The villagers believed this was a sign the gods were punishing Baba Yaga and as she was also childless people began to suspect she was a witch. Fearful that this was indeed a warning from the gods, the villagers drove her away without mercy. Friends and neighbours and even her own family chased her off with insults and blows, leaving her for dead in a forest brook. Her marriage was annulled so she also lost the man she loved.

Miraculously, Baba Yaga was saved by a band of real witches and quickly became one of them. One day, on her way to a secret gathering, she learnt that her husband had remarried and was now the father of two boys and a pretty little girl! Baba Yaga's heart filled with a fierce hatred for the new family. The gods had deprived her of the joy of being a mother surrounded by children, a husband's love and the kindness of a family. They would pay dearly! Baba Yaga planned to make the whole world pay for her misfortunes. No one would be safe, especially not those children!

Baba Yaga became a sour-tempered witch full of resentment. She was taught the ancient rituals of black magic and how to concoct strange potions using secret herbs. After a few years, she became the most skilled of the witches and was elected to be the leader of the coven. Once sure that she had mastered the art of sorcery completely, Baba Yaga began to get rid of her sister witches. They were no longer any use to her so, one by one, she disposed of them with her poisons.

Now her hour of vengeance had come. Baba Yaga snatched her former husband's children and killed them in the forest. Next, she threw a poisonous mushroom into the village's water supply and watched smugly as most of her old friends died. Then she sent a plague to finish off the survivors.

Baba Yaga captured Gunther, her former husband, as he lay weak and dying, and tore out his heart. She then put a spell on the heart, so that it kept on beating, and placed it in a jar of thick liquid. She had had her revenge! Now Gunther's heart would beat for her alone until the end of time.

Baba Yaga was so thrilled with her magic powers that she began to commit countless atrocities in the surrounding villages. She stole children and boiled them alive to make potions and elixirs. Faced with this terrible threat people fled their homes and abandoned their villages. Soon Baba Yaga found herself alone in the vast forest. In order to satisfy her growing desire for destruction she began to attack the animals that lived around her. Once all the mammals had fled she only had to get rid of the birds. That was why she was out poisoning them. She cursed the spring and hated all the signs of new life stirring in the forest.

AMOS DARAGON

The old woman finished her murderous task and returned to her cottage. As she came in she called out: 'I'm back, Gunther dear! I do hope you weren't bored!'

The witch was talking to the heart of her former husband. She talked to him all the time.

'I've been out feeding the vermin, dear. There won't be so many tomorrow, you'll see! Oh yes, Gunther, I promise you, there'll be fewer and fewer. We'll have peace soon when all this singing finally stops. Now don't sulk, Gunther. Are you angry? Are you thinking of your second wife? Yes, it's true, she was a beautiful singer – until I cut out her tongue and killed her. Do you remember how she screamed? Ah, it fills me with joy whenever I think of it! What wonderful memories we share, Gunther... such wonderful memories!'

Baba Yaga walked towards a big wooden table that almost filled the cottage. The witch sat down heavily on a chair and looked round the room. There was a bed with filthy covers; a bubbling cauldron hanging in the soot-blackened fireplace and an untidy shelf where books, ointments, human bones, children's skulls, small desiccated animals and other knick-knacks lay jumbled together. Gunther's heart, imprisoned in its jar of greenish liquid, stood beside the window's dirt encrusted panes.

'We're a bit tight on space, aren't we, Gunther?' she exclaimed, looking at his jar. 'We'd better do a bit of cleaning... hmmm... I think the last thing I cleaned was your son's skull after I cut his head off. Oh, that naughty boy didn't want to let me! Hee hee hee! He really was a wonderful little boy! Brave too! He even spat in my face before I cut his throat! Oh yes, Gunther, he was brave just like you!'

There were three loud knocks on the cottage door. The witch jumped up with a little cry of panic. Startled, she looked towards Gunther and whispered: 'Who on earth can be knocking at my door? What should I do, Gunther? What's that? Oh yes! That's a good idea!'

The old woman seized a rusty knife and hid it behind her back. As she walked towards the door she heard another three knocks.

'I'm coming!' cried the witch, trying to make her voice pleasant. 'I'm all alone and I'm old and can't move very fast...' Baba Yaga opened the door slowly. Its hinges made a loud grating noise that frightened away all the birds that remained in the woods. Before her, some distance away, sat a grey wolf looking straight at her. The witch glanced left and right before asking the animal:

'Is it you who wants to see me, you filthy creature?'

'Yes it is I who wishes to see you,' replied the wolf in a deep voice, pronouncing each word very clearly.

'A talking wolf!' cried the astonished witch. 'Gunther, you ought to see this! A talking wolf has come to see us! I hate wolves...'

As she spoke, Baba Yaga pulled out the knife and with a speed and agility remarkable for her age threw it at the wolf. The animal caught the blade in its teeth and hurled it back at her. It struck the witch hard in the shoulder and she fell down howling with pain.

'Look what that wicked wolf has done to me, Gunther! Did you see? Oh, you vile wolf! I'll rip the skin off you...' The creature didn't move a muscle, but waited for the witch to get back on her feet. Baba Yaga stood up and pulled the knife from her shoulder. She was bleeding profusely.

'What do you want with me, you miserable creature?' she demanded. 'Do you enjoy hurting old ladies? Does it amuse you to terrify a defenceless woman?'

'You are most entertaining,' replied the wolf with a hint of a smile. 'I have come on behalf of my master, to ask for your help.'

'Never!' screamed the witch. 'I never help anybody and I'm not about to start now! Go tell your master that I'm an old woman; tell him to leave me in peace.'

'Can you really be Baba Yaga?' asked the wolf. 'The most feared witch in the whole world?'

'It's too late for compliments now!' the old woman snapped rudely. 'Clear off!'

'Very well then' said the wolf, 'I just thought you might still be interested in killing children... my mistake. I'll leave now.'

'Just a minute!' cried Baba Yaga. 'You have been extremely rude... First you disturb me, then you stick a knife in my shoulder and now you plan to leave without telling me why you're here! Come in, you wretch.'

'My master warned me not to come too close to you lest I be turned into soup...'

'Your master is a wise man! Who is he?'

'He is called Loki.'

'L...L...L...Loki,' stammered the witch. 'You are Loki's wolf? Loki, the god of Fire and Strife?'

'Yes, indeed,' agreed the wolf, nodding his head slowly.

'Well, that changes everything,' cried the witch, shame-faced. 'Do you hear that, Gunther? Loki's wolf has come to call on us. Isn't that lovely? What a wonderful surprise!'

'My master has a job for you. He wants you to kill two children who irk him. A straightforward task, don't you think?'

'Quite straightforward! A simple task!' cackled the witch arrogantly. 'Tell me, why does Loki want to be rid of the little rascals?'

'That does not concern you,' responded the wolf drily. 'You just kill them.'

'And what can I expect in return?' simpered the old woman.

'Nothing except his good opinion!'

'And if I refuse…?' asked the witch.

'His wrath will pursue you into the next world!'

'Well, isn't that wonderful!' said Baba Yaga angrily, through gritted teeth. 'Do you hear that, Gunther? We're going to do Loki's work for free. Aren't we the lucky ones! What a pleasure it will be to serve a god who is so generous to us! Tell me, mister wolf... What do they call these adorable little chicks whose throats I must cut?'

'They are two boys. One is called Amos Daragon and the other is Beorf Bromanson…'

CHAPTER TWO

SPRING IN UPSGRAN

All the villagers were assembled in the inn down by the little harbour in Upsgran. The windowless wooden building rang with joyous singing. The Beorites had gathered to celebrate an important occasion: it was Amos' birthday! The remains of an enormous banquet held in his honour were strewn all over the place in an unholy mess. Beorf was presenting his friend Amos with a huge four-tiered cake filled with nuts and honey and adorned with thirteen candles. The crowd clapped wildly and burst into the traditional birthday song. Amos blew out the candles to another volley of applause. The young mask-wearer was presented with a fine set of clothes which had been woven by the women of the village: a pair of long, comfy, waterproof boots, a handsome Viking helmet and a strong travelling bag made from an old boat sail.

Banry, Beorf's uncle and the village chief, began to speak: 'It is a great pleasure for us to celebrate your birthday today. Our resounding victory over the goblins and the dragon of Ramusberget Mountain has given our people self-confidence again. This is all thanks to you, Amos, and we are profoundly grateful!'

The excited crowd clapped and chanted: 'Long live Amos! Long live Amos!'

'I know,' continued Banry, 'that we can never replace your father, who was killed in Berrion, or your mother, who was captured and sold into slavery by the goblins. So far we have searched in vain to find her but we will go on searching. The best present we can give you today is our pledge to find her. But, in spite of the sorrow and anguish of your loss, we want to ask you a great favour.'

As he spoke, the Beorites had quietly begun to cut up and hand round the cake. In spite of Banry's solemn speech no one was able to resist the sight of the honey-drizzled nuts and the smell of the blueberry icing. They handed a plate to Banry who continued speaking as he ate:

'Your encounter with the Brising in the forest of Ramusberget revealed the curse which has afflicted our race. You told us about the necklace of Brisingamen and about the war between Odin and Freyja and how we might remove the curse. We must go to Freyja's island and beg her mercy. Will the Goddess of Fertility allow us to see our children grow up once more? We hope so!

Now, here is my request: we should like you to go with us on this adventure. Your help would be invaluable to us and we were waiting for the right moment to persuade you…'

Amos rose and answered: 'You know that I don't need much persuading to set off on another adventure. However I would like to have a few days before I give you my answer. I need to consult my teacher, Sartigan, to see what he thinks…'

'Take all the time you need!' replied Banry. 'I'm sure he won't see any problem.'

The party resumed and the sound of traditional folksongs and dances floated across the village well into the night.

The next morning Amos struggled to rouse himself to go to visit Sartigan. He hadn't slept much and the Beorite music was still dancing inside his head. The young mask-wearer and his friend Beorf were staying with Banry. Taking care not to wake them, Amos ate bread, some fruit and a hard-boiled egg before setting off for the forest.

Sartigan, his old teacher, was waiting to begin the day's lesson. A former dragon hunter, he had miraculously survived being imprisoned in a block of ice for almost a thousand years. He was now the young mask-wearer's guide, helping Amos to develop his full powers.

Sartigan was a little eccentric and Nordic people found his appearance quite strange. He had slanted eyes and wore his two metre-long beard wound around his neck like a scarf. Even in winter he only wore an orange monk's robe and walked barefoot. His breath smelt like an old sock. However he was a wise man and Amos loved to listen to all that he had to say.

Since their return from Ramusberget, Sartigan would see Amos every morning and Beorf three afternoons each week. The young mask-wearer was being taught how to control his special powers, while Beorf was training for hand-to-hand combat.

Both boys had made good progress. Amos' skill at controlling his magic was increasing and each day he discovered more about the powers the Masks of Water, Air and Fire gave him. Beorf fought well. He was more agile now, he moved more efficiently and struck with greater accuracy. Thanks to his regular training, Beorf had even lost a few kilos in weight and was now very fit.

Sartigan had taken up residence in a neat little cabin outside the village in the middle of the forest. He found Upsgran far too lively and noisy. The Beorites had helped him to build a little log cabin near a pretty lake and in this beautiful place Sartigan could practice his meditation without being disturbed. He had learnt to speak the Beorite language quite well, but Amos and Beorf always wore their crystal elf-ears during lessons.

The elf-ears, a gift from Gwenfadrilla, the queen of the forest of Tarkasis, allowed them to speak and understand any language. The boys had tried several times to listen to Sartigan's instructions in the Beorite language, but without the crystal ears they only understood about half of what he said.

Sartigan's cabin was also the ideal place to keep the dragon's egg. The boys had brought it back in great secrecy from the dragon's lair in Ramusberget. No one else knew of its existence. Dragons had disappeared from the face of the earth hundreds of years before and the little creature asleep inside its shell must not be allowed to fall into the wrong hands. Amos had just thwarted Baron Samedi in his attempt to restore the rule of the Ancient Ones – the dragons. Never again should anyone have the opportunity to use the dragons' strength for evil purposes.

In Sartigan's cabin the egg was close to hatching. Separation from its mother had disturbed the egg's development. In order to break out of its shell the little dragon was waiting to be placed on a bed of burning coals. Sartigan reckoned that if it was subjected to great heat the creature could be born in just a few seconds.

As usual, Amos entered his teacher's cabin without knocking and found Sartigan waiting patiently. The boy greeted him and went to look at the egg. He stroked the shell gently before putting on his crystal ears:

'We should make it hatch! What do you think?'

'Or perhaps we could throw ourselves off a cliff or shoot arrows into each other!' exclaimed the old man.

Amos laughed aloud.

'It would be suicide and you know it!' insisted Sartigan. 'When the dragon gave you this egg, you took it with the best of intentions. You were convinced that if this innocent little dragon was raised to be good it could co-exist with humankind. Unfortunately a dragon isn't the same as a lamb. A sheep gives us wool but a dragon brings chaos. Its deepest urge is to destroy, dominate and conquer. That is in its nature! A dragon is opposed to peace; it is the embodiment of war. Even in infancy it can kill a griffon or annihilate a battalion of well-trained soldiers. But you know all of this... I've explained a hundred times already.'

'Yes, I know,' said Amos with a smile, 'but when you talk about dragons you get so wound up that your face turns red. It's funny to see you like that!'

'You rascal!' exclaimed Sartigan, roaring with laughter. 'I have never had such a talented and impertinent student as you! Now prepare yourself. We are going to start with a solid hour of active meditation.'

'Can I ask your advice, master Sartigan?' asked Amos with some hesitation.

'Of course, my young friend,' replied the old man seriously. 'What do you want to ask?'

'The Beorites will be setting off for Freyja's island soon and they've asked me to go with them. I don't know what to do because of my mother... she is a prisoner somewhere and I need to find her. I know she is still alive! I have been using my magic powers to send her communication bubbles with messages of reassurance. Unfortunately she cannot reply to let me know where she is! Should I set off in search of her without any clues or tracks to follow, or should I go with the Beorites to help them as best I can? I am torn between love for my mother and my friendship with Beorf and the people of Upsgran. I don't want to refuse the Beorites, but I don't want to abandon my mother to her fate. If I go to Freyja's island people will think...'

'People will think...', said the old man slowly, emphasising each word. 'It is not important what I think of the choice you have to make, and other people may think what they like. Let me explain: Once, when I asked my master what I should do to please other people, he told me to follow him into the village. My master rode on a donkey and told me to keep hold of the reins and lead him into the market square. When we arrived I heard some men saying, "Look at that mean old monk riding a donkey while his poor novice walks! Monks are always so selfish!"

'The next day we repeated the exercise, but this time I rode the donkey. The very same men grumbled loudly,

"That novice has no manners! Fancy making his master walk when he's so old and exhausted! Young people today just don't know the meaning of good manners!"

'The third day we went back to the village, pulling the animal behind us. This time the response was: "Just look at that monk and his novice! They are too stupid to ride on the donkey to save their feet! Monks aren't as clever as they used to be!"

'On the fourth day we both rode the donkey only to hear: "Look at them... they don't care about their poor donkey! Never trust a monk!"

'By the fifth day, just to prove how ridiculous it could get, we both carried the donkey. From all sides we heard: "Monks are completely mad! Just look at what they're doing. Monasteries... more like lunatic asylums!" Do I need to explain the moral of my story?'

'No need,' laughed Amos. 'I understand. Whatever I do, people will think what they like... no two people will have the same opinion two days running.'

'Never do anything just to suit what other people may think. You must feel for yourself which path you ought to follow. I am not here to show you the road but to accompany you on your way.'

'Thank you!' replied Amos. 'You always give me such good advice.'

'Let's get on with our meditation now,' said the old man, taking up a cross-legged position in readiness.

'Just one more thing before we start,' giggled Amos. 'Did you really carry the donkey on your back?'

'Sshh,' said Sartigan gently but firmly. 'We'll talk about that later...much later!'

Just after he had left Sartigan's cabin, Amos passed Beorf going for his lesson. The fat boy looked relieved:

'Am I glad to see you! I forgot my crystal ears. Can I borrow yours? I'll take great care of them.'

'Yes, of course. Sartigan's use of Beorite is improving all the time but not quite enough to teach.'

'Well, are you coming with us to Freyja's island?' asked Beorf, carefully putting the elf-ears into his bag.

'Yes, I think so. I'm going to do what seems best for the moment.'

'I'm so pleased!' shouted Beorf as he headed off. 'I'm already late and Sartigan will be mad at me again! Fancy going fishing before it gets dark?'

'Good idea. See you later!'

Amos went down to Upsgran's little harbour. He could see Goy and Kasso Azulson on the deck of the biggest drakkar (a longship). They were arguing with Banry. The two brothers were evidently quite worked up. Kasso was the drakkar's navigator. Unlike Goy and every other Beorite he was very thin, ate little and never gained an extra ounce in weight. Goy was an accomplished warrior and an unbeatable rower. He had a stocky build with powerful shoulders and a thick neck, and ate without any worries about the size of his belly. Kasso was an excellent archer whereas Goy wielded a sword with great skill. Together the brothers made a formidable team even though they always seemed to be arguing.

'Look, Banry, according to our maps there is no more sea!' cried Kasso animatedly.

'No more sea!' exclaimed Goy, wide-eyed.

'No. There's nothing,' Kasso continued. 'We'll just fall off the end and get eaten by the great serpent!'

Amos jumped aboard.

'Hello everyone!' he said cheerfully. 'What's going on Banry? You all look fed up...'

'That's right! We are!' said Banry, the village chief and captain of the ship. 'We shan't be able to get to Freyja's island. According to the directions the Brising gave us it's outside our world... we'd fall off the edge before we could get there.'

'Eh?' said Amos in astonishment.

'Let me explain,' said Banry. 'We Beorites have the same beliefs as our Viking neighbours: that we live in an enormous ash tree, called Yggdrasil, whose high branches prevent us from seeing Åsgard, the kingdom of the gods. In the sky is a huge palace made of logs where endless feasting goes on. We call this Valhalla, where the souls of brave warriors find everlasting rest when they die. Do you understand?'

'That sounds like a very interesting and poetic way to imagine the world,' mused Amos.

Banry continued, 'In the middle of the tree is a flat disc surrounded by water. This is where the land and the mountains of mankind's world are – the land we live in! If we sail too far, well... we'll fall off the edge! Then Vidofnir, the great serpent who guards it, would devour us. The serpent creature sees to it that we don't go further than the gods allow. Yggdrasil's roots go down deep into an icy hell that is the land of giants. That is where the souls of cowardly or dishonourable warriors go when they die.'

'So you can see why Freyja's island is not on our charts,' added Kasso. 'We shall never be able to get there. It is beyond our world in a place where we are not allowed to go!'

'And we would be eaten by Vidofnir!' added Goy, anxiously.

'But surely there must be some way to reach the island,' murmured Amos.

'We would need Skidbladnir!' laughed Banry. 'That's the gods' ship. It was built by dwarves and can sail on land, on sea or through the air. It is big enough to carry all the gods and a whole army of Vikings. It can also fold up into the size of a handkerchief. The legend says it looks like a winged dragon and that its sail is always wind-filled so it can travel at incredible speed.'

'Unfortunately, we only have this ship!' interrupted Kasso. 'Our drakkar is nothing like Skidbladnir!'

Amos thought for a while before he replied: 'Well, Freyja's curse means that your children die young, so the Beorites will soon die out, but on the other hand it seems we will all die if we try to reach her island. Even if we did get there, we don't know that she will listen to us...'

'What's to be done then?' asked Goy in bewilderment.

'I think that the world is like a reindeer and that we are blind!' continued Amos.

'I don't understand what you mean,' said Banry, intrigued.

'It is one of Sartigan's stories: a reindeer was placed in front of four blind men who were each asked to describe the creature. The first man stepped forward and touched its antlers, straight away he said that it was like a tree. The next touched its tail and assured them a reindeer was like a rabbit. The third man felt its leg and hoof and declared that it was just like a horse. As for the fourth, he put his hand inside the creature's mouth and described it as a slimy, stinking monster.'

'I know what you're getting at!' cried Goy. 'It means never trust a blind man. Is that it?'

'No, that's not it,' laughed Amos. 'It means that we are just like those blind men – our understanding of the world is limited to our own perceptions. We think we know the truth, but we have no true concept of what a "reindeer" really is. As we cannot see our universe as a whole we get things wrong!'

'Well, I know what a reindeer is!' declared Goy, proudly.

'For the love of Odin be quiet, Goy,' said Kasso. 'Amos is just using it as an example... a metaphor...'

'Oh... I see now,' said Goy very solemnly, scratching his head. 'I get it now. I understand.'

'So do you think we've got it all wrong and that we should try our luck?' asked Banry.

'I think that we might be surprised,' said the young mask-wearer.

'I think you're right,' cried Banry. 'We won't be put off by fear. We'll make new charts and we'll get to the island even if we have to fly there! Kasso, prepare the drakkar. We set off a week from now. I assume you're coming with us, Amos?'

'Oh yes!' declared the boy. 'It should be an interesting journey!'

CHAPTER THREE

INTO THE UNKNOWN

The Beorites were an orderly and traditional people. For their previous expedition to the Viking lands of Ramusberget Banry had chosen the crew. Once again the village chief looked to the village of Upsgran for his crewmen.

Helmic the Insatiable rushed to the inn to be first to put his name at the top of the list of volunteers. He was very different from the other Beorite men! It was less to do with his strength or courage than his appearance. Unlike the others, he was bald and clean-shaven. He had small ears and piercing eyes, a sizeable belly, bulging muscles and an insatiable lust for adventure and exploration. He was an ideal fighter and travelling companion and he was always Banry's first choice.

From the long list of volunteers Piotr the Giant was also selected. Part man, part grizzly bear, he was nearly two metres tall and had the strength of a demi-god and the courage of a whole Viking army. His long moustache was plaited, giving him the look of a wild barbarian. In fact, though he did weigh 200 kilos, he was the gentlest of giants.

The Azulson brothers, Goy and Kasso were also chosen; Kasso for his navigation skills and Goy for his prowess at rowing and fighting.

Banry also picked Aldred the Axe for his physical strength and his unfailing good temper. In battle, with his axe in hand, he transformed and became a veritable tornado.

Rutha Bagason, known as the Valkyrie, was the only woman chosen for the adventure. She could fight with the strength of three men and was thorough with everything she did. It was her job to provision the ship because she thought of everything and was always prepared for the unexpected.

Hulot Hulson, also known as Big Mouth, was the hero of Ramusberget. The Beorite who was said to have killed the dragon with a single sword stroke did not put his name forward. Although continually boasting of his bravery when faced by the dragon, he refused to take part in this new adventure saying he had 'the 'flu'. Everyone knew that Hulot was just scared, but Piotr, Aldred and Goy added his name to the list as a joke. To Hulot's utter dismay Banry chose him to go, declaring that the drakkar could not possibly sail without their great hero! Beorf and Amos completed the crew. Geser Michson, known as the Stone Marten, and Chemil Lapson, known as Fairy Fingers, had also taken part in the Ramusberget adventure and both accepted Banry's decision not to choose them with regret. Many other Beorites, good fighters and brave seamen all, were also left behind.

The drakkar was as heavily laden as a merchant ship. Beorites were notorious for travelling with enormous quantities of food. There were dried sausages, salt fish, honey and nuts, whole sides of smoked wild boar, huge quantities of potatoes, all kinds of pâtés, terrines and tarts as well as apples, jars of blueberries, hard-boiled eggs, barrels of wine, water, cakes, biscuits and various vegetable purées. There was enough on board the drakkar to feed an army!

As well as all this food there was armour, shields and helmets, a variety of spears, a large communal tent, oil lamps and navigational equipment. This left little room for the crew, so it was lucky there were few of them.

In the days leading up to the departure, Amos noticed a big black crow that always perched on the same branch and watched them closely. Its eyes never left the ship. Was this a good omen or not? The crew would soon find out.

The day before they were due to leave, Amos went to see Sartigan for his last lesson.

'I've got a bad feeling about this trip,' Sartigan confided. 'Someone wishes you ill. I can't really explain what I mean but take great care. You are very astute, Amos, but there are devious forces in this world. Someone will set a trap for you, I can feel it. Beorf is under threat, too. You must keep a cool head and act cautiously. Don't let yourself be drawn in!'

Amos was rather shaken by these words but promised to be cautious and to warn Beorf to be on his guard, too.

'One more thing,' Sartigan added. 'You must take the dragon's egg with you. I've decided to go away for a little while.'

'Where will you go, Master?' asked Amos, much surprised.

'You have your path to follow and I have mine,' replied the old man quietly but revealing no more.

'Well you take care of yourself, too! I don't want to lose you, I've still got a lot to learn.'

'No, you won't lose me. I'm going to cancel your lesson for today. When I see Beorf this afternoon, I shall give him the egg and tell him to hide it on board the drakkar; he's good at that kind of thing. It's big, but I'm sure he'll find some place to hide it.'

'Won't it be very risky to take the egg with us!'

'Yes, perhaps, but let's say it's a calculated risk. Go now and good luck, I shall be thinking of you!'

'Goodbye! You be careful, too!' called Amos as he left the little cabin.

The ship set sail on a cool spring morning. The whole village gathered by the harbour to wave farewell to the adventurers. The wind filled the sail and they set off towards the rising sun. The Beorites made a fine spectacle as they rowed! Banry stood at the helm with Kasso and his sea charts beside him. On the port side Beorf and Aldred the Axe were the front oarsmen, Helmic the Insatiable was in the middle with Rutha the Valkyrie behind. To starboard were Amos at the bow of the ship with Goy and Hulot in the middle and Piotr the Giant at the rear. The journey began cheerfully, the rowers keeping time to a rhythmic chant.

Early in the afternoon Kasso asked Amos for help. Banry took the boy's place at the front of the drakkar while the navigator took the helm.

'Look, Amos…I've just found something very strange in this old ship's log which belonged to my great-grandfather. According to him, he and his crew came across a huge impenetrable fog barrier. He has written that it is guarded by the "Grey Man" and that no human is allowed to sail through it. Do you know anything about this Grey Man?'

'It doesn't mean anything to me but I'll have a look...' answered Amos, going to find his bag. He took out a big black book: Al-Qatrum. It was a book he had borrowed from Beorf's father's library and it contained a mass of information about strange and unusual creatures to be found all over the world. Amos had already discovered all sorts of useful information in it.

It was how the young mask-wearer had found out about the Howling Hounds on his way to Upsgran. These big treasure-guarding dogs had vanished before his eyes and turned into a magic necklace. Without Al- Qatrum Amos would never have understood what had happened! He had given the necklace to Beorf who wore it all the time.

Amos skimmed through the pages of the book until he found an entry about the Grey Man. He was a giant known by several names: Far Liath, An Fir Lea or Brolaghan who was supposed to guard a place known as 'The Great Fog Barrier'. His body, formed of thick sea fog, appeared when ships approached. His aim was to sink all ships to prevent humans from crossing the world's threshold. According to Al-Qatrum it was impossible to succeed against this colossal creature. Over time many good sailors had tried to sail past the Grey Man and through his wall of fog, but none had returned to tell the tale.

'I don't like the sound of that!' exclaimed Kasso when the young mask-wearer told him what he had found. 'Can you think of a plan, Amos?'

'No. We will obviously meet this Grey Man on our travels and we have to succeed where others failed. I must give it some serious thought...'

'You'd better do that, Amos. At the speed we're going I wouldn't be surprised if we see him in a few weeks' time. That might seem a long time but it doesn't give us much time to prepare for such a meeting. You know that our drakkar has to travel where no Beorite has ever set foot before and...'

'What did you just say?' interrupted Amos suddenly.

'I said no Beorite has ever set foot where...' Kasso began to repeat when he was interrupted again.

'My dear friend,' the boy exclaimed with a big smile, 'that's just what we have to do: to get through the wall of fog and persuade the Grey Man to let us go on!'

'What?' asked the astonished navigator.

'Just wait and see,' said Amos with a wink. 'I've got a plan now. I'll explain later.'

CHAPTER FOUR

OTARELLA

They had been travelling for a week and still the drakkar sailed onwards. The Beorites had eaten little and had been rowing very hard so they were becoming bad tempered. They were hoping to land somewhere soon as they needed a few days of eating and sleeping. Kasso had spotted a tiny island on his charts where they might rest, but there was no sign of it in the vast ocean. 'Are we nearly there?' cried Piotr the Giant. 'I'm sick to death of rowing day and night.'

'I can't understand it,' answered Kasso, shrugging his shoulders. 'The island should be right in front of us! We should be able to see it from here.'

'If we had a decent navigator we might have been on the blasted island by now!' complained Goy.

'Just watch out, brother... if it's trouble you want, I'm ready for you!'

'We're lost!' cried Hulot in panic. 'We'll never find land, we'll never see Upsgran again! I'm sure we've been going round in circles for the last two days!'

'No we haven't!' Banry butted in. 'We're not going round in circles and everything is just as we thought it would be. We've a calm sea and a good wind and we'll soon be able to rest!'

'I'm sure we're lost and it's your fault, Kasso!' insisted Hulot, getting more and more agitated as he rowed. 'You've lost the knack of navigating, that's what's wrong! Freyja is against us and we're all going to die at sea!'

'Shut up, Hulot!' ordered Banry. 'You're doing nothing for our morale. We have enough food for a month. You are not going to die of hunger!'

'I'll climb the mast,' said Kasso. 'Take the tiller, Banry. I'll be able to see better from up there.'

Kasso scanned the horizon carefully but he could see nothing in any direction. Then, just as he was about to climb down, he caught sight of something floating not far from the drakkar.'

'I can see something,' he shouted. 'Turn to port, Banry. It looks like... yes, it looks like a body floating in the water!'

The ship headed towards where Kasso was pointing. To their great astonishment there was indeed a body: the body of a young mermaid!

Pulling her on board, they laid her carefully on the deck. The Beorites had never seen a mermaid before; they stood staring at her knowing neither what to do nor how to help her. They were used to fighting the hideous mermen and so were amazed by the mermaid's delicate beauty. Instead of legs she had a magnificent fish tail with pointed fins, she also had incredibly long blue-black hair and lips that were the richest crimson against her snow-white skin. She was dressed in a simple garment made of seaweed with a belt of white shells and a leather purse, and around her neck was a delicate chain with a little wooden chest hanging from it. The mermaid was having great difficulty breathing.

The crew's stunned expressions reminded Amos of his own first encounter with a mermaid. It had been at the Bay of Caves in the kingdom of Omain. There Crivannia, the princess of the sea, had given him a white stone and told him to go to the forest of Tarkasis. It was thanks to her that he had become a mask-wearer and that he had met Beorf.

Amos leant over the mermaid to see if he could hear her heart beat. It was beating – but very faintly! He tried to revive her by whispering in her ear while using his magic powers to force air into her lungs. Immediately she began to breathe more easily.

As the mermaid came round Amos gazed into her deep black eyes and was instantly bewitched. His heart beat faster, his hands began to shake and his mouth felt dry. At that moment, for the first time in his life, the young mask-wearer knew that he was in love.

The mermaid spoke in a musical voice:

'Hello. My name is Otarella. Who are you, young man? Who are all these men? Where am I?'

'One question at a time, Otarella!' replied the boy tenderly. 'My name is Amos Daragon. These men are my friends and you are on a longship. We've just fished you out of the water! You were floating unconscious, just drifting.'

'I can't remember what happened,' Otarella declared, trying to sit up.

'Stay where you are until you get your strength back,' advised Amos. 'You'll soon remember...'

'You are very gentle, young man. I was fortunate to be rescued by such kind souls! And you are very good looking.'

Amos turned as red as an apple and the whole crew burst out laughing. They poked gentle fun at him. Beorf whispered in his ear:

'You're even better looking when you blush like that!'

'Stop it, Beorf, that's not funny!' Amos protested, pushing his friend away. 'If I'm red it's because... because I've caught the sun! That's all!'

'That's strange! There's no sun today! In fact I'd say it was rather cloudy.'

'Shut up, Beorf! Mind your own business and just row. We'll never get to the island with this nonsense!'

'Right you are then, my handsome friend. I'll keep quiet!' sniggered Beorf.

'Land ahoy! I can see land!' yelled Hulot at the top of his voice.

'We're saved! We're saved!'

'Shut up Hulot! Just row!' ordered Banry. 'How can we be saved when we were never in danger! Kasso was right. The island is just over there. Come on lads, we're nearly there!'

It was a great relief for the whole crew to set foot on the island. The Beorites were fine sailors but they were much happier on dry land. The big tent was quickly erected and the provisions unpacked. Hulot began to cook while Amos and Beorf prepared a place for the young mermaid – after all, she couldn't walk.

'Can I help?' asked Otarella. She was standing beside them on her own two feet! Beorf gaped in astonishment. What on earth had happened to her tail!

Otarella was wearing a long skirt made of flimsy, dark blue material and a pair of pointed shoes. Amos rubbed his eyes and stammered:

'But what happened to your tail? You've got legs now!'

'Of course I have,' answered the mermaid innocently. 'We mermaids can adapt ourselves to life on land as well.'

'That's incredible!' exclaimed Amos in astonishment.

'I've never heard that!' cried Beorf, amazed. 'But if mermaids can do that, Amos, how come Crivannia was hiding in a sea cave instead of going further afield? She was being chased, wasn't she?'

'Don't nit-pick!' retorted the young mask-wearer angrily. 'Otarella must know what she's talking about. She's a mermaid, isn't she?'

He turned towards her and apologised: 'You'll have to excuse Beorf, he can be a bit stupid at times!'

'Not at all, it doesn't matter,' said Otarella, gently putting her hand on Amos' shoulder.

'What?' cried Beorf, 'You're calling me stupid!'

'That's enough!' snapped Amos coldly.

'Right!' said Beorf brusquely, 'I'm off then. I'll see you later.'

Amos didn't try to stop him, instead turning his attention back to Otarella. They made a campfire a little way away from the others. Amos had spread out a big cover by the fire where they ate together, watching the magnificent sunset. The two lovebirds chatted for hours, learning more about each other as they talked. Otarella was so beautiful that Amos drank in her words like a man dying of thirst. He began to feel as if time itself was standing still.

After their gargantuan meal the Beorites took themselves off to the big tent to sleep. Beorf came to say goodnight to his friend, but Amos was so absorbed in what Otarella was saying that he didn't even notice.

'What's going on?' asked the mermaid innocently in her tinkley voice. 'Has everyone gone off to sleep?'

'Yes. They'll probably sleep for at least three days now,' Amos told her. 'We shall be quite alone for some time. I hope you won't get too bored with just me to talk to!'

'You're not the kind of boy a girl gets bored with!' smiled Otarella coyly. 'Tell me, did you say you were a magician?'

Amos couldn't recall telling her about his magic powers, but Otarella was so pretty, he quickly dismissed this passing thought.

'Yes. I am a mask-wearer.'

'That sounds interesting, what kind of magic can you do?'

'I was chosen by the White Lady to keep the world in balance!' Amos boasted. 'It's not so simple. I have to find four masks that are linked to the elements, plus sixteen stones of power. The more stones I have the greater my powers over air, fire, water and earth will be!'

'And where are these wonderful masks then, oh, great magician?' asked Otarella mischievously.

'I haven't got them. Or at least, I do have them but I can't show them to you. They have become part of me. I found the Mask of Air first, then the Mask of Fire and then the Mask of Water. I only have three stones so far: one for each element! They are part of me, too.'

'That's a very interesting way to come by magic, Gunther dear!' murmured Otarella.

'Why did you call me Gunther? Have you forgotten my name?'

'No!' answered Otarella, flustered. 'I haven't forgotten. It's just that, er... my brother is called Gunther. I feel so relaxed with you that for a moment I got you mixed up with him. I'm sorry!'

'That's strange,' said Amos innocently. 'I thought all mermaids were women.'

'Well, yes and no. It all depends on their sex at birth,' stammered Otarella in confusion. 'But what about you? Tell me more about yourself. I want to get to know you better.'

Amos told her everything. He told her about his adventures, his childhood in the kingdom of Omain and all about his great battle with the Dragon of Ramusberget.

This gave Baba Yaga, as Otarella, plenty of time to get hold of the big knife she had hidden under the rug and to think out her plan of attack. She planned to slit his throat, hide his body somewhere on the island, take on his appearance and wait for the right moment to kill Beorf. Just as the witch was about to take aim, the young mask-wearer told her about the dragon's egg. She stopped just in time, slipped the knife back under the rug and asked teasingly:

'A dragon's egg? You've got a real dragon's egg? I

think you're just saying that to impress me. You are charming, Amos, but I don't believe it!'

'But it's true!' cried Amos. 'I've got it here with me. It's on the ship. Come on, I'll show you! Oh no, I can't, Beorf's got it! If I know him, he'll have hidden it somewhere secret when we landed.'

'So we'll have to wait for him to wake up to see this wonder,' sighed Otarella. 'How tiresome!'

'I'm so sorry, truly I am,' groaned Amos.

'It doesn't matter. It won't do you any harm to wait!' grumbled the sweet young mermaid.

'What did you just say?'

'I said… er… I don't mind waiting!'

'Well, I must get some sleep now, I'm exhausted,' yawned Amos. 'Are you coming? I'm sure Beorf will have made up a bed for you in the tent.'

'No, I'd rather sleep in the water. I am a mermaid, remember!'

'You won't disappear overnight, will you?' asked the young mask-wearer anxiously.

'No, I'm still too weak to go back to my sisters. Go. Sleep well. I can't wait to see you again tomorrow.'

'Same here,' said Amos awkwardly. 'It's the first time... oh, I don't know how to say this...'

'I understand!' Otarella placed her finger on his lips to stop him speaking. 'Off to sleep now!'

'Yes, I suppose that's for the best. Good night!'

Amos' heart was full of joy as he went into the tent thinking that he had found his soul mate! He felt at peace with himself. He had never felt so happy to be with anyone like this before. He would have given Otarella the moon, the stars and the whole world on a silver platter if he could.

The mermaid lingered outside and, stroking her pendant, she murmured: 'See what a big heart I have, Gunther! I could have killed him with one thrust of my knife. But no, he had to tell me about a dragon's egg. Just imagine what we could do with a dragon, Gunther! I'm all a-tremble just thinking about it. I hope that young fool isn't leading me on a wild goose chase. If these Beorites think they are going to sleep for three days I've got bad news for them: they'll be up tomorrow first thing! I need to get Beorf to show me that egg. It won't be easy; he's not as stupid as Amos and not so easily led. He's more down to earth and less taken in by my beauty! It's nice to think I'm still attractive to young boys! Gunther, do you remember when we first met? You were about the same age as him! Ah well.

'We've got work to do, Gunther! Let's go a bit further inland, I've got potions to make and spells to prepare. I've got to make myself beautiful for tomorrow, too. Otarella's a lovely name for me, isn't it? You like that name don't you, Gunther? Yes, I know it was your second wife's name... I do hope you're not jealous!'

CHAPTER FIVE

DISCORD

The sun rose over the island. The crew's loud snoring made the ground vibrate, but this time Amos had remembered to bring wax earplugs. He had learnt how to overcome this problem on his first trip with the Beorites! He knew you had to come prepared if you wanted to get any sleep with a bunch of snoring man-bears.

The young mask-wearer had slept well. He felt warm and comfortable snuggled under his bedcovers. But soon he began to feel too cocooned. He felt warm, in fact a little too warm! Amos tried to turn but couldn't. He opened his eyes sleepily.

'Spiders! Spiders everywhere!' yelled Kasso in panic.

The mask-wearer was instantly wide awake as though he'd had cold water thrown over him. He couldn't move a muscle. In the semi-darkness of the tent he could see thousands of spiders moving about. They were everywhere! Large and small, thin and long! They were busy spinning the big tent into a giant cocoon. Amos could see that everyone had been so trussed up that they couldn't even wiggle a toe.

Kasso was shouting to wake the crew. In a few seconds the whole tent was in uproar. The Beorites, imprisoned in the spiders' silk, howled in disgust but could not break free.

Banry, red faced with fury at being trapped so easily, tried to bite the spiders. Hulot wept, while Helmic fought like the devil to get free. There was nothing they could do – they were trussed up like sausages. Beorf bellowed:

'Do something, Amos! Can't you burn these damned spiders!'

The young mask-wearer quickly thought it through. Fire would certainly burn the spiders, but with them the tent and all its occupants! He needed his arms to raise the wind, and water wouldn't be much help either.

'I can't do anything Beorf! I really can't do a thing. I need someone to free my arms!'

At that very moment Otarella rushed into the tent and flung herself at Amos. From the folds of her skirt, she drew a large rusty knife and quickly freed the boy. The young mermaid took him by the hand and led him out of the tent.

'Thank you so much, Otarella!' he cried.

'You can thank me later,' cried the beautiful heroine, 'but do something!'

'Right!' replied the mask-wearer, taking up a strange oriental pose.

'Now we'll see exactly what your magic can do, young show-off,' she muttered to herself.

Amos stood with his legs apart and his hands clasped in front of his face as if he were praying, He concentrated and took several deep breaths. Suddenly he flung his arms out wide and gave a great cry. A powerful gust of wind engulfed the tent and carried it several metres into the air. The spiders were instantly thrown all around onto the rocks and into the trees. The smallest landed in the ocean or far across the island.

In order to stop the spiders coming back, Amos stamped his feet three times and ran right round the trussed-up Beorites. A great ring of fire rose up in his path making a burning wall the spiders could not cross.

Amos used Otarella's knife to free Banry. In a few minutes all the Beorites were freed from their cocoons and ready to leave the accursed island. Amos extinguished the wall of fire and the spiders had gone!

'Well done, Amos!' said Beorf. 'We're in your debt once again! It's a while since I saw you doing any magic. You've definitely got it under much better control now!'

'I've got Sartigan to thank for that!' answered Amos

proudly. 'Anyway, we should really be thanking Otarella. She is the reason that we're still alive. Those spiders would have sucked us dry if she hadn't been there!'

'Yes, of course,' agreed Beorf. 'Thank you, Otarella!'

'It was nothing,' replied the mermaid. 'I was asleep in the water when I suddenly had a sort of premonition. I got out of the water, heard shouting coming from the tent and rushed in to save Amos so he could do something to help you. He's so clever!'

'That's strange,' said Beorf looking at the mermaid closely. 'You were sleeping in the water yet your hair isn't wet. Does it dry very quickly?'

'What are you getting at, Beorf? She saved our lives. Why would she lie?' said Amos.

'No, it's all right,' sighed Otarella sadly. 'Your friend doesn't know me like you do, so it's not surprising that he doesn't trust me. My hair dried in the heat given off by Amos' circle of fire just now. Are you satisfied?'

'Almost,' replied Beorf, 'but that doesn't explain why you have a steel knife. Steel rusts and would surely be destroyed by salt water! I thought you told me that all mermaids' weapons were made of coral and sea shells, Amos?'

'That's enough, Beorf!' cried Amos. 'I don't understand why you have to keep on at Otarella. Perhaps you are jealous because she's more interested in me than she is in you? Not all girls are like Medusa, just waiting for a chance to betray us!'

'I never said that,' snarled Beorf. 'And leave Medusa out of this. She was a sweet Gorgon and she was nicer than this liar Otarella!'

'Apologise for what you've just said!' yelled Amos. 'Apologise or...'

'Or what?' shouted Beorf, rolling up his sleeves. 'I'll knock you down before you can even think of using one of your magic spells.'

'You! You're far too slow and predictable to be a threat to me,' sneered Amos, nastily.

They had almost come to blows when Rutha interrupted them sharply: 'Instead of fighting you could come and help load the drakkar! Settle your differences later or we could leave you here on the island if you'd prefer it! Then you could kill each other in peace! Right now we need some help. Come on!'

Stepping back a little, Beorf snarled and bared his teeth at Amos before turning towards the ship. The mask-wearer followed in his footsteps, accompanied by Otarella.

'I am so sorry,' the mermaid murmured. 'This is all my fault! I'll go away and leave you with your friend.'

'No, Otarella, it's not your fault, it's Beorf. He's a numbskull! I think he's making things up about you because he's jealous. You see, we're like brothers. We're always together, always going off on new adventures and now... well, I suppose I haven't been paying him much attention and he's taking it badly.'

'The important thing is that you trust me,' whispered Otarella taking hold of his hand.

The drakkar nosed out to sea, and the Beorites, who hadn't had enough sleep, cursed as they began to row. Amos took his place by Beorf at the front of the ship and the boys set to work in icy silence. Neither spoke or glanced at the other, pretending indifference.

The Beorites had installed Otarella comfortably in the centre of the ship near the mast. She sat wrapped in thick furs, with her long black hair flowing in the breeze. Amos couldn't help looking at her out of the corner of his eye. She was so beautiful! Beorf was also watching her, wondering who she really was and just why she was lying so brazenly.

Several hours passed until Banry suddenly ordered a well-earned break and the rowers stopped. The wind was blowing hard enough to speed the heavy drakkar onwards.

The Beorites were thirsty. They opened one of the barrels of drinking water and found several spiders floating on its surface. The water looked brown.

'Filthy creatures!' cried Helmic. 'They've drowned in it and poisoned our water. It's undrinkable!'

'We must check everything,' ordered Banry. 'Have a look at the wine and the food and do it carefully... our lives depend on it!'

To their consternation they discovered that nothing was edible. The barrels of wine and beer were also contaminated. All the meat was covered in white patches and the tightly sealed jars were open. Everything was spoilt and Banry ordered that it be thrown overboard. The crew did as they were told but looked deeply upset.

'This is a terrible blow,' sighed Rutha. 'We're in trouble now. How can we survive at sea without food or drinking water? We can catch fish and we can always try to control our enormous appetites but we must find water!'

After consulting his navigation charts Kasso announced there was a string of islands to the west, about seven days' sailing away. Would they find drinking water there? He had no idea.

The Beorites looked at their captain and awaited his orders. He said that they had three choices. First, they could go back the way they came, back to Upsgran. With a bit of luck they would get there, dehydrated but alive. Second, they could return to the island of spiders and look for water there. Third, they could go on to the islands that Kasso had found with the risk of finding no water there.

'As you know, our laws state that we must take a vote to decide what to do,' declared Banry.

Helmic exclaimed, 'If you decide to go back to Upsgran I shall throw myself overboard! I'd rather die in action than go back home dragging my tail like a beaten dog. Whether I win or lose I don't stop in the middle of an adventure.'

'Well you can get on with it yourself then!' cried Hulot. 'It's better to get back to Upsgran alive, take on more supplies and start again. It would be stupid to risk our lives just for your ridiculous principles. We'll just have to get to Freyja's island a few weeks late, that's all! There's no hurry.'

'I think we should go on!' Kasso reasoned. 'We've got a good steady wind! Let's take our chances and head west.'

'I must remind you that we've all got to agree before we do anything,' said Banry. 'Lower the sail, Goy. We're staying here till we have a consensus!'

'I want to go back to Upsgran,' said Piotr the Giant. 'I'm starving!'

'We're wasting time!' snapped Rutha. 'You decide, Banry. Don't worry about getting everyone to agree!'

'We have to respect our laws,' said Aldred the Axe, weighing his words carefully. 'Banry is our captain and the leader of our village: he must apply the rules strictly or we'll have no control!'

'I agree with my brother,' said Goy. 'The Azulson family is unanimous. We should go on!'

Banry turned, 'What do you think, boys?'

'I think we should go on and take our chances,' Amos declared confidently.

'I drank some water just after we set off and I don't feel too good,' Beorf cried in anguish. He leant over the side of the drakkar and was violently sick. The Beorites rushed to help him and laid him down where Otarella had been sitting. She took his place next to Amos.

'Your friend looks in a bad way,' whispered the beautiful mermaid. 'I do hope it's nothing serious!'

'So do I,' said Amos hanging his head. 'I feel so bad now about what happened this morning. We've never quarrelled before! We usually get on so well. I don't know how it happened.'

'It's nothing to worry about,' the young mermaid reassured him. 'I don't know anyone who hasn't quarrelled with their best friend at some time or another. There are always misunderstandings between friends. I just hope he'll give me a chance!'

'Yes, you're right, Otarella! Stay here,' said Amos getting up. 'I'll see if there's anything I can do for him.'

Otarella nodded and smiled. As she sat alone at the ship's prow, she stroked her pendant and muttered to herself: 'Yes, off you go, you little runt. Go and see what you can do for your dying friend! Oh, poor Beorf! What a way to die. All alone at sea, abandoned by everyone. How awful, don't you think, Gunther? That big strong boy has no idea what's coming. My poison is very strong and there is no antidote. It's already too late! He doesn't know it yet but his blood will begin to turn black and his body will soon be covered with hundreds of suppurating boils. He will suffer! His skin will dry out and fall away in tatters; his bones will break one by one but his heart, lungs and brain will keep on working. You know what that means, Gunther, don't you? He'll be in agony! He will share the fate of many of my younger victims.

'Obviously, I shan't be able to use a manimal's body to make the "essence of child" which enables witches to fly, but I shall still have young Amos for that! Now, don't you fret, Gunther, I'll get Beorf to tell me where he hid the dragon's egg before he dies. No, I didn't see him bring it on board this morning but everything has been thrown overboard now so it can't be far. But where is it? I've looked everywhere. It won't be long now, Gunther! Just be patient.'

CHAPTER SIX

THE BEORITES WAIT

It was almost sunset and still the boat had not moved. The Beorites had been arguing all day long! Hulot wanted to turn back to Upsgran while Helmic insisted they carry on to the archipelago of islands. 'Man-bears are a very democratic people,' Amos told Otarella. 'This kind of dispute often happens. One side has to give way before they can move one way or the other. A good captain or leader must make sure the laws are respected. That's what Banry is doing.'

Beorf seemed really ill and the crew was gripped by thirst. It was generally agreed that the Beorites should sleep on the problem so they prepared themselves to sleep at sea. Before he settled down, Amos went over to see Beorf one last time. He looked peaceful and seemed to be in a deep sleep. The mask-wearer spoke quietly to him:

'I don't know if you can hear me, Beorf, but I'm really sorry I called you stupid. It was cruel of me and I didn't really mean what I said. You are my best friend and I hope you always will be! Sleep well.'

Amos went back to the front of the ship to lie down. Otarella had made space for herself next to him.

'How is your friend?' she asked.

'I think he's a little better,' replied Amos. 'He's sleeping now.'

'But that's impossible!' muttered Otarella crossly.

'Impossible. Why?' asked the mask-wearer.

'Oh, I meant to say...' faltered the beautiful mermaid, 'I meant... er... it's impossible that he shouldn't be better! He's such a strong boy that he's bound to be back on his feet soon! In fact, if you don't mind, I'll sit up with him for a while. I'm not tired and someone should stay with him.'

'Very well,' replied Amos with a yawn. 'Wake me up if there's any change. Good night!'

'Good night and sweet dreams!' said Otarella smiling kindly as she moved to Beorf's side.

She sat down next to the sick boy pretending to watch over him. She waited patiently until all the Beorites were snoring then the witch bent down to Beorf's ear and hissed:

'I can't understand why you're still breathing, you filthy wretch! Your skin should be covered with boils by now and you shouldn't be sleeping either, you should be screaming in pain! I have underestimated you and the stamina of your disgusting race. But that doesn't matter now because you're going to show me where you've hidden the dragon's egg! Wake up! Wake up you filthy rat!'

'What is it?' groaned Beorf. 'What's happening? Where am I?'

Otarella held her knife to his throat and demanded: 'Where have you hidden the dragon's egg? Tell me!'

'What's going on? Otarella, why have you got a knife at my throat?'

'I'm not a mermaid, you little idiot!' declared Baba Yaga. 'I am a witch and I'm will cut you into little pieces if you don't tell me where you hid the egg!'

'But you must be raving, Otarella!' cried Beorf. 'You're much too beautiful to be a witch! Witches are horrible, aren't they?'

'You're an idiot!' exclaimed the exasperated witch. 'I have powers, great powers. I can change the way I look whenever I want. I bewitched your friend Amos so that he fell madly in love with me. It was child's play! I fooled everyone except you, but that doesn't matter now because you're going to die! Tell me where the egg is and I'll make sure you don't suffer.'

'I'll tell you,' agreed Beorf, trembling. 'But first, I want to see your real face.'

'Mmm. The last wishes of a condemned man!' sneered Baba Yaga. 'That's so sweet! Very well, you fool, feast your eyes.'

Checking that the crew was still asleep, Otarella mumbled some incomprehensible spells. The beautiful girl disappeared before Beorf's eyes and was replaced by a repulsive, deeply wrinkled old woman with white eyes, foul breath and thin grey hair. Baba Yaga spoke:

'Are you happy? Look at me! Have a good look because I am the last thing you will see before you die! Where did you hide the egg? Tell me!'

'I hid it,' said Beorf, 'I hid it in Amos' shoe!'

'What?' she cried. 'But a dragon's egg is too big to fit into a shoe!'

'And an old witch can't fit into the skin of a beautiful girl, either!' cried Amos as he stood up at the front of the ship.

'Surprise!' cried Beorf as he smashed his fist into the witch's jaw.

Baba Yaga fell over backwards and spat out her two remaining front teeth. As she got to her feet Amos struck her with a ball of flames that set her clothes on fire. For a moment the witch seemed to dance on the spot but then hurled herself overboard to douse the flames. A little cloud of steam rose, followed by a cry of relief.

Piotr the Giant quickly reached out and fished her out by the leg. Baba Yaga struggled and spat out the foulest of curses. Goy walloped her on the back of the head with an oar and the witch immediately lost consciousness.

When she came to, Baba Yaga found herself tied to the top of the mast. She was sitting on the crosspiece, trussed up like a sausage. The midday sun was hot and the drakkar was speeding onwards.

'What's going on? Aren't you ashamed to treat an old lady like this, you band of ruffians?'

The crew roared and howled with laughter. Beorf climbed up the rigging and took a seat beside the prisoner.

'Good morning, pretty Otarella! Although you're not so pretty this morning! Did you have a bad night?'

'I don't understand,' screamed the witch. 'You shouldn't be here making fun of me. You should be dead! Explain or I'll skin you alive!'

'You're in no position to threaten me!' sneered Beorf. 'Can you see that very large Beorite down there? His name is Piotr and he doesn't like old shrews like you. He's been told to keep an eye on you. Mind your manners or I'll tell him to come up and...'

'No need for that, young man!' she answered hastily. 'No need at all! You've got the better of me, you and Amos, you wretched creatures!'

'I must admit you played your part well. We fell for your mermaid trick back on the island. Until we went to sleep in the tent things were definitely going according to your plan. Amos fell for your trick completely and I'm sure he was very much in love with you.'

'That's only to be expected with good looks like mine!' the witch scoffed.

'It was your gold chain with the little chest pendant that gave you away.'

'Where is it? It's not here any more!' howled Baba Yaga. 'Give me back my pendant!'

'Later. I'll finish my story first,' said Beorf calmly. 'I remembered seeing that necklace somewhere before and then it came back to me! I'd seen it hanging round a crow's neck in Upsgran. The crow that Amos had pointed out! Now, there's a coincidence!'

'So what?'

'So, after your little tête-a-tête with Amos, I waited for him to come back to the tent to sleep. I tackled him about you and despite his pig-headedness in believing me to be jealous, I reminded him about the necklace, the pendant and the crow. He suddenly woke up! Your spell over him was broken! We talked things over logically and decided that you couldn't be a mermaid! But we didn't know what you had planned for us! Only when Amos mentioned your fascination with the dragon's egg did we begin to hatch a plan. It seemed obvious that you wanted to...'

'But what about the poison?' she snarled. 'You were poisoned weren't you?'

'Well, no actually, but I am a good actor! Next morning we realised what your wicked plan was when we saw all the spiders. We warned the crew and while Amos and I pretended to argue, Rutha checked the food and found that it was all poisoned. We loaded it all on board and set off to find out what you were up to. We just pretended to find out it was poisoned at sea! Then we acted out a fine scene of despair for your benefit and I just stuck a finger down my throat to make myself sick at the right moment!'

'But you still have no food or drinking water!' snarled Baba Yaga nastily. 'You will still die!'

'I don't think so,' replied Beorf, smirking. 'The archipelago is just a day's sailing from here. Kasso's grandfather mapped all the islands himself, so we know we'll find drinking water there and plenty of game to hunt. Beorites certainly do have laws, but with us it's the village chief or the captain of a drakkar who makes decisions for the crew. We're not so stupid that we'd just hang around at sea to die! Helmic and Hulot led you a merry dance with their disagreements! You fell right into our trap! We played our parts well, didn't we?'

'Aaaaah,' screamed the witch. 'I hate you... I hate you all!'

'Yes, I'm sure you must!' said Beorf, feigning sympathy. 'But now it's my turn to ask you some questions. What do you want from us and why did you try to kill us?'

The witch told him that the god Loki had sent a grey wolf to give her this task. She said she had only agreed to do it for fear of reprisal. Loki was a treacherous god who loved to make trouble whenever he was bored. He took great pleasure in humiliating mortals and getting the better of them. Baba Yaga insisted that she had pleaded – she was only a poor old woman and they shouldn't be mean to someone of her age!

Beorf gave her a knowing smile. No one becomes a witch overnight; he knew that it takes a dark soul to practice the dark arts. Witches were ruthlessly cruel child killers. Not content with just cutting their victims' throats, they liked to torture them first, delighting in their screams. Sometimes children were dropped into boiling oil or roasted on a spit. At other times the wicked creatures ate their young victims. Witches are almost immortal and the only way to get rid of them is to burn them alive. That was how Beorf's parents, Evan and Hanna Bromanson had died in Great Bratel. Yaune the Purifier had falsely accused them of witchcraft and had his soldiers burn them at the stake.

Beorf climbed down the mast to tell the crew what he had learnt.

'By Odin!' exclaimed Banry. 'If Loki is against us... we're in trouble!'

'Loki certainly isn't stupid,' said Amos after a few moments' thought. 'If we are successful in persuading the goddess Freyja to lift her curse, perhaps relations between her and Odin will improve. Once the gods stop quarrelling with each other, they can concentrate on fighting evil instead! I don't think Loki would tolerate a reconciliation between Freyja and Odin. If these two gods were united they would become too powerful. They could crush him like a worm.'

'I think that's exactly it!' agreed Kasso.

'That's why he sent this witch after us!' concluded Banry. 'She was supposed to wreck our expedition and cut us into pieces. That means...'

'It means that mermaids are all wicked witches and we've got to keep our eyes peeled for them!' cut in Goy, sounding pleased with himself.

'No,' replied the captain. 'It means that the gods must believe we have a chance of convincing Freyja and they are taking our expedition very seriously! It's excellent news!'

A loud cheer rose from the crew.

'Let's head for the archipelago and some fresh supplies!' shouted Helmic, dancing on the bridge. 'We're a match for anything once our bellies are full!

The crew went back to their oars and Beorf went up to Amos and said:

'How are you? How are you feeling?'

'I feel so stupid,' Amos replied through gritted teeth. 'How could I let myself be taken in so easily? I can't believe that I fell in love with that old harpy! When I close my eyes I see Otarella, so sweet and pretty, and I'm overwhelmed!'

'Don't worry,' said his friend reassuringly. 'Everyone makes mistakes, me especially! In this case you were powerless. Her spell was too strong.'

'Thanks for saying that, Beorf. I don't feel quite so stupid now.'

'And after all, not everyone is lucky enough to be as handsome as you!' Beorf teased. 'Even witches choose you for their sweetheart!'

'Oh no, don't start!'

'Okay... I'll shut up. All the same, it must be hard being so handsome!'

'You're not going to give up, are you? I can see I'll have to put up with your sarcasm for weeks to come.'

'Years, more like!' laughed Beorf cheerfully. 'Many, many years...'

CHAPTER SEVEN

LOKI'S REVENGE

rakkars are flat bottomed and specially designed to be able to land easily, no matter where. So the Beorites had no problem in getting onto the island. They quickly set up camp, dividing the tasks between them. Amos and Beorf were responsible for finding drinking water. Just as the whole crew was about to set off in various directions, Baba Yaga, who was still trussed to the top of the mast, yelled at them:

'Don't just go off and leave me here! You can't leave me alone!'

'And why not?' mocked Banry, grinning broadly.

'Because Loki will take his revenge on me!' replied the witch. 'I must go with you. My life is at stake! I'll be safe with you! If you leave me here, Loki will kill me as punishment for failing in my mission. You wouldn't want to have an old lady killed, would you?'

'You can't be trusted one bit,' Helmic shouted up to her. 'If Loki is your master, you'll just have to talk to him! Your problems are nothing to do with us!'

'Very well then, you bunch of cowardly stinking vermin! But give me back my pendant! If I'm to die I need to take it with me!' Baba Yaga howled.

'You're taking nothing,' replied Amos. 'Your pendant and gold chain are very safe in my pocket and that's where they're staying! We've tied you up to the mast and you won't be coming down until we can put you in prison in Berrion or Great Bratel to stand trial! Until then it's safer to leave you on your perch up there to take the air.'

'And don't think you can cause us any trouble,' jeered Hulot Hulson. 'A few months ago I killed a dragon single-handedly with one blow of my sword! Let me tell you all about it. At Ramusberget it was, we were attacking the hideout of some dangerous bloodthirsty goblins, when all at once...'

'Oh, he's off again!' exclaimed Piotr, putting his hand over Hulot's mouth. 'Just set off and I'll make sure she stays quiet!'

The Beorites spread out over the island laughing heartily. Baba Yaga stayed behind, tied fast at the top of the drakkar's mast. As she saw the men move off she began yelling wildly:

'Goodbye Amos Daragon! May the curse of Baba

Yaga go with you! Goodbye Gunther! And goodbye to this rotten world!'

Amos turned round and shrugged his shoulders. Beorf was walking beside him. 'You look worried.' he said.

'No, not really,' Amos replied. 'I was just wondering what the witch is afraid of. I was thinking about Loki too. But enough of that! Let's just concentrate on what we're supposed to be doing now! There's no point in worrying just yet.'

'I was wondering why that pendant means so much to her.'

'We'll take a look at it when we get back if you like,' suggested the mask-wearer.

The Beorites had been gone from the drakkar for about an hour when a grey wolf stepped out of the forest and calmly sat down nearby. Baba Yaga's blood froze in terror.

'Tell your master that everything is going very well! My plan is working like a charm. I've fooled them all! Go quickly! I don't want them to see you, it would spoil my plan!'

'Your plan!' scoffed the wolf calmly in a deep voice. 'What plan might that be? Here you are, tied up, unable to move, mocked by mere children and held captive by man-bears. What plan?'

'It would take too long to… er… explain. You… you wouldn't understand,' stammered Baba Yaga, great drops of sweat forming on her face. 'Leave immediately, I've got everything well under control! Things will work out… you'll see!'

'No. Nothing will work out,' said the wolf. 'Loki has told me to eliminate you which is precisely why I'm here! You have seriously endangered my master by speaking of him to the Beorites. The man-bears are Odin's favourite creatures; he must not know that Loki is involved in all this. You've made too many mistakes. I am sorry!'

'No, no,' begged the witch. 'I'll sort everything out. Just set me free and I'll kill them all. Be kind, nice little doggie. No, no, not fire! No! You can't burn an old lady. Noooooooooo!!!'

As they searched for water Amos and Beorf reached the top of a little hill on the other side of the island.

The boys stopped at the edge of a cliff to look out to sea. Below them they saw a huge, three-masted ship that had been stranded on the rocks, its tattered sails fluttering in the breeze. It was easily ten times the size of their drakkar. It must have been trapped between the cliffs and the waves for many, many years.

'I wonder what happened to the crew?' said Beorf.

'Probably all dead,' answered Amos. 'The sea's very rough here! You'd have to be an excellent swimmer with luck on your side, to have got out alive…'

'Let's hope that my uncle Banry can avoid a disaster like that!' sighed Beorf looking worried.

'We've already seen worse things,' said Amos, trying to cheer him up, 'We've beaten an army of gorgons, destroyed a Naga wizard, put Yaune the Purifier's spirit into a chicken, faced an army of goblins and defeated a dragon!'

'Hmm. Not bad considering you're only thirteen and I'm fourteen! Just imagine what stories we'll be able to tell when we're fifty or sixty!'

'No one will believe us!' laughed Amos. 'They'll wag their fingers and call us madmen!'

Although tired from the sea journey and their long walk, the two boys laughed fit to split their sides. Amos laughed so much he ached and Beorf was gasping for breath and had tears rolling down his cheeks. After several minutes Beorf took some deep breaths and as he wiped his eyes, said:

'I wonder who's lit the fire?'

'What are you talking about?'

'Look, over there! There's a plume of smoke. It must be near where we landed. There's quite a lot of smoke; it must be a very big fire…'

'Oh, no!' cried Amos. 'That's what Baba Yaga was so afraid of, Beorf! What's the best way to get rid of a witch?'

'Burn her!' Beorf answered, pleased he knew the answer. Then he suddenly yelled: 'Now I understand! It's the ship! The ship's on fire!'

Instantly turning himself into a bear, Beorf charged down the hill at full speed. Amos couldn't keep up with him but ran as fast as he could towards the burning ship.

By the time they reached the shore it was too late to do anything. Huge flames leapt from the drakkar. The blackened remains of the witch dangled nightmarishly from the mast. Her flesh had melted and her skull was visible. There was no doubt that she was dead.

Beorf's roar had brought back the Beorites, who gazed in silence as the flames engulfed the drakkar. Only Hulot dared open his mouth:

'How many days would it take to swim to Upsgran?'

His only reply was a great thump on the back of his head from Piotr.

Amos leaned closer to Beorf and whispered in his ear: 'Just tell me the dragon's egg isn't on board! Please... tell me it's not on the drakkar!'

Beorf didn't move but bit his bottom lip nervously. After a few seconds he answered: 'I hid the egg between the hull and the deck of the ship. It's being roasted right now.'

'If what Sartigan told me was true,' murmured Amos

slowly. 'Then we're about to witness the birth of a dragon! The egg was mature and ready to hatch. The heat will make the dragon wake up and break out of its shell!'

'Do you know how to teach a dragon to behave nicely?' asked Beorf hesitantly.

'No, replied Amos. 'But we shall have to find out very quickly. According to Sartigan dragons are dangerous even when they are little. We need to warn the crew that we're about to get a surprise visit...'

'But how shall we tell them?' asked Beorf, who was worried about the Beorites' reaction.

'We'll have to improvise!' said Amos swallowing hard.

'On you go then,' Beorf exclaimed, uneasy. 'You're the mask-wearer, after all! I'm sure they'll take more notice of a handsome lad like you!'

Amos sighed and asked the crew to gather round. Nervously, he told them the part of the Ramusberget adventure he and Beorf hadn't mentioned before. He told them about meeting the dragon and the present the creature had given him. Finally he said:

'Beorf and I brought it back home to Upsgran on the ship. We didn't tell anyone about it. We thought the little creature had a right to live and that if it was raised by good people it might become an incredible creature which could do good.'

'But Sartigan told us that dragons' souls are evil,'

added Beorf. 'They are created by forces of evil in order to do evil and, according to him, it's a mistake to think that one day they might be a force for good.'

'But when Sartigan had to go away he gave the egg back to us. I suppose there was less chance of its being in contact with a source of heat on a boat...'

'And so,' concluded Beorf, 'I hid it between the hull and the deck of the drakkar. That means, unless there's a miracle, we're going to witness the birth of a dragon any moment now. Any questions?'

All heads turned to the burning drakkar. The mast fell, bringing with it the remains of Baba Yaga. Then the Beorites heard a cry or a moan coming from the embers. Instinctively everyone stepped back. A second, much louder, cry froze their blood. To their astonishment a small head emerged from the flames. A four-legged lizard, about two metres long with big wings folded across its back and a very long tail leapt onto the shore. The creature already had long pointed teeth and powerful claws. The little dragon gave a cry of hate, coughed and, looking at the Beorites, it licked its chops. Beorf leaned over to Amos:

'I think he's hungry! What do dragons eat?'

'Manimals and humans!' answered Amos with a half smile. 'He's looking at a banquet!'

CHAPTER EIGHT

TAMING THE DRAGON

Amos felt something move in his pocket and took out Baba Yaga's pendant. The little wooden chest was vibrating as if about to explode. The mask-wearer hurled it away as hard as he could. As it fell the pendant returned to its normal size and a large chest landed on the ground with a crash. 'What on earth's happening?' asked Beorf.

'I don't know!' cried Amos.

'First a dragon is born and then a magic chest appears. Things are certainly moving fast around here!' declared the young Beorite, overwhelmed by all that had happened.

A sudden flash of inspiration came to Amos. He shouted to the Beorites:

'Give all the food you've found to the dragon! It will keep him busy and give me time to do something… and do keep an eye on him. I've got an idea!'

The Beorites did as he asked. They had fruit and roots but very little meat. The new-born dragon accepted his first meal disdainfully. He began by devouring the hares and pheasants and then, rather reluctantly, started on the roots.

While he was doing this Amos ran to the chest. He had guessed that Baba Yaga had used it to carry her possessions. When the witch died the spell that had reduced its size to a pendant had obviously been broken. Perhaps the chest held the solution to his problem!

Inside it he found bottles and phials, a large book and – to his horror – a glass jar containing a human heart! And the heart, sealed in a greenish liquid, was still beating…

Amos immersed himself in Baba Yaga's spell book. He turned the pages feverishly, murmuring:

'Reduce… reduce… that's got to be the answer. Reduce, but where? No! Or shorten, maybe? Shrink? Come on Amos! Find it!'

After several long minutes he found what he was looking for. He tore the page from the book, rummaged in the chest and seized a phial filled with white powder. He ran back to the dragon, yelling to Beorf:

'There's an empty jar in the chest and a cork stopper next to the heart. Just look and you'll understand what I mean! Make some holes in the cork and bring me the jar please. Quick, as fast as you can!'

'Right!' shouted Beorf.

The baby dragon had greedily finished his meagre meal. The Beorites formed a semi-circle around him and kept him at bay with their weapons. The creature had no experience of how to rid himself of these big warriors who stood in his way. His blood began to boil and he was getting more and more furious as each second passed. The young dragon turned, glancing at the ocean behind him. No way out in that direction. The choice was simple. Either the man-bears or the salt water! The fire beast's instincts favoured fight over flight. He was now ready to reduce them to porridge!

When the little dragon turned to face them he saw the Beorites had moved back a little. Amos stood before him, alone. The dragon bounded forward, ready to bite his head off. The mask-wearer just had time to throw a handful of white powder over the creature and utter a strange chant from the witch's book:

'Aton na bar ouf, oug ignakar kilk!'

The dragon's sharp pointed teeth never reached Amos. In less than a second the creature was reduced to the size of a salamander. Amos seized it by the tail and showed it to the Beorites with a laugh:

'Well, here's our dragon! I think he'll give us less trouble now! Beorf, the jar please!'

'Here you are,' said the boy, handing it to him.

Amos slid the little creature into the glass container and sealed the jar with the pierced cork.

'Phew, that's one problem solved!' he sighed. 'Now we can feed it on insects. I don't know how long it will stay this size though! The page from the witch's book didn't say...'

'We'll soon find out!' replied Beorf. 'If it's the same as the pendant we should have a few weeks' peace.'

'Yes,' agreed Amos. 'Perhaps the spell is only broken by the death of the sorcerer.'

'That's fine, but now for our other problem!' said Banry, scratching his head. 'We've got to find some way of getting off this island and going home. We can't continue our journey to Freyja's island without a ship!'

'For the time being,' said Aldred the Axe, 'I think we should go back into the forest. We've got to find food and a place to sleep.'

'I saw some caves just west of here that would make a good shelter!' suggested Helmic.

'Good thinking,' exclaimed Banry, rubbing his hands. 'Even when things don't turn out exactly as we'd like, there's always hope! Let's take a look at these caves and see if we can make them our headquarters. Then we can concentrate on finding food.'

'What about the dragon?' asked Hulot nervously. 'Can't we just drown it? Then we'd be rid of it.'

'No! That's not a good idea!' said Amos. 'I'll take responsibility for the creature.'

'And I'll be its guardian...,' declared Beorf, taking the

jar from Amos' hands. 'I'll take care of him! After all, it's partly my fault we've got him with us.'

'That's decided then!' agreed Banry. 'Let's go to the caves. We'll take the witch's chest with us and maybe Amos can take a look at what's in it and perform some more miracles! Lead the way Helmic, and we'll follow you!'

As the crew set off Hulot grumbled to himself: 'I never even put my name on that wretched list in the first place. I should be back in Upsgran. What am I doing here? We're all doomed.'

Ignoring Hulot's grumbling, Beorf glanced at the dragon. The creature didn't look too happy either!

'What made you think of shrinking the dragon then?' he asked Amos.

'Well,' answered the young mask-wearer, 'witches always need ingredients to cast their spells. Don't you remember how Lolya always needed hens, candles, leeches and other things for hers. I guessed that Baba Yaga's pendant chest probably held all her needs. I guessed that the reducing spell might work for dragons too and luckily it did! Fortunately her book wasn't that difficult to understand!'

'Well done!' said Beorf proudly. 'Sartigan always says you should follow your instincts.'

'And take chances.'

'I mean "calculated risks"!' they both cried in unison, laughing wildly.

'It's that heart in the jar that scares me. Have you seen it? It's still beating. It's horrible!'

'It really gives me the creeps. I'll study Baba Yaga's book and have a look through the chest. Perhaps we can find out more.'

With Helmic leading the way they quickly reached the caves. They were at the bottom of the hill that Amos and Beorf had climbed earlier. It seemed an ideal spot to set up camp. The Beorites settled in and then headed off in all directions to gather food. Banry asked the boys to guard the camp.

While they waited for their friends, Amos had a good look at the witch's chest and Beorf went exploring deeper into the caves. The young mask-wearer studied the spell book carefully. He found recipes for poisons and magic formulae but nothing to show why a heart should be in the chest. The heart was suspended in a sticky, translucent liquid that filled the jar. Amos thought about Lolya as he studied the book and tried to understand it. She would have been a great help to him now.

Beorf came back from his explorations empty-handed. He sat down heavily alongside Amos, saying:

'There's absolutely nothing in these caves! I had hoped to find something interesting: ancient drawings, runes or even some treasure. But you can't always be lucky. Sometimes a cave is just a hole in the rocks. How's our friend in the jar?'

'He's asleep,' said Amos. 'I gave him a few grasshoppers to eat and he seemed satisfied. If anyone had ever told me that one day I'd be walking around with a dragon in a jar, I'd never have believed them!'

'What are we going to do?' Beorf asked. 'We'll have to get off this island. We need another ship or our adventure comes to an end right here and now.'

'I can't see any way out of this either,' sighed the mask-wearer. 'Nothing seems to work...'

'I wonder what Sartigan would say?' Beorf wondered aloud.

'He'd say,' replied Amos imitating Sartigan's voice, 'in the darkest hour the light shines brightest!'

'If only we had horses that could gallop over the water and then we wouldn't need a ship! But that's not possible.'

With a wide grin, Amos turned to his friend, 'Beorf, you're a genius!'

'Eh? I haven't a clue what you are talking about! But if you say I'm a genius – you must be right!'

CHAPTER NINE

THE KELPIES

A mos began looking through his things and took out his crystal elf-ears. 'I've had an idea that might save us. You stay here and keep an eye on things. I'll be back in a minute!'

'And what am I supposed to do if the dragon goes back to his original size?' asked Beorf.

'Just keep him talking and try not to get eaten!' shouted the young mask-wearer, already some distance away. 'Tell him one of your jokes and send him to sleep!'

'Right,' grumbled the boy. 'So, I've got to sort out any problems myself!'

Amos soon reached the little beach with the burnt-out drakkar. He waded into the water until it was up to his waist, closed his eyes and concentrated hard. He was using the powers of his Mask of Water to try to send a message through the waves to the Kelpies. He neighed and tossed his head towards the water three times.

These strange actions created a kind of vibration that seemed to wrap around his message rather like an envelope around a letter. The message rolled off on a wave, deep into the ocean.

The mask-wearer repeated these strange actions several times. Fortunately luck was on his side. A shoal of herring caught the vibrations from one of his messages and amplified it towards some salmon. They passed it to an enormous blue whale which after a while passed it to some cod. The message rolled onwards: to a lobster, a crab, a hermit crab and a large eel before finally reaching its destination in the ear of the Kelpie chief.

An hour had passed before Amos stepped out of the water. The sea was icy and he was shivering violently. He turned to his magic powers once more. This time he used the Mask of Fire to help raise his body temperature. Drops of sweat soon formed on his forehead as if he had a high fever. He was no longer cold! Sartigan had shown him how to make the magic flow through his body. That was how his teacher managed to walk barefoot throughout the winter without getting frostbitten toes. Sartigan himself was not a mask-wearer and did not possess power over the elements like Amos, but could accomplish this feat through perfect control of his thoughts.

Amos felt better and relaxed his concentration.

Thinking that his attempt to communicate with the Kelpies had been unsuccessful, he wondered what to do now? He would have to think of something else! But, just as he was about to leave the beach, the sea began to change.

Amos saw twenty or so Kelpies emerge from the waves. These creatures of the deep ocean, part man, part horse, were around two metres tall and walked on their hind legs. They had the heads, flowing manes, long tails and hooves of a horse, but their torsos and arms were like those of a human.

Checking that his crystal ears were properly in position, Amos began to speak with the sea creatures:

'Greetings,' he said, pawing the ground three times with his right foot. 'I am glad to see you. Thank you for coming!'

'Amos Daragon, mask-wearer!' declared the leader of the group, neighing wildly. 'You are a friend to the Kelpies. We owe you our respect and help.'

'I need your help badly!' cried the boy opening his mouth wide and baring his teeth like a horse. 'We are prisoners here. Our ship was destroyed by fire, but we need to get to Freyja's island.'

'But you must know that humans cannot cross the Great Fog Barrier?' said the Kelpie politely as he galloped on the spot. 'The Grey Man will not allow you to go through it.'

'I know that,' said Amos, pawing the water as he spoke. 'But we must try our luck. The future of the Beorite race depends on it. Can you help us?'

'Your destiny is for you to decide. I will not stand in your way,' continued the Kelpie, tossing his mane. 'I only want to warn you of the danger. I am here because you called for help. Ask and I will listen…'

'Thank you,' replied the mask-wearer, snorting noisily through his nostrils. 'On the far side of this island lies a wrecked ship. Can you help my friends and I to get it afloat again so that we can continue our journey?'

'We will do that for you – we don't need any help!' the Kelpie assured him. 'We shall work tonight and tomorrow you shall have your ship. Your friends can rest. I hope that is not too long for you?'

'That is far better than I dared hope!' exclaimed Amos as he bucked this way and that. 'How can I thank you? Can I help you in return?'

'That time will come, mask-wearer,' the creature assured him, 'I shall see you tomorrow at sunrise on the other side of the island.'

'I am greatly in your debt,' said the boy, making a deep bow. 'Come, my brothers,' ordered the Kelpie as he plunged back into the water. 'We have work to do!'

Amos took off his crystal ears and quickly went back to the camp. When he got to the caves he found the Beorites sitting round a fire eating greedily.

'You've got back just in time!' cried Hulot. 'Another two minutes and you would have gone hungry!'

'We leave at dawn tomorrow!' cried Amos smiling proudly.

'What's that? We're leaving?' cried Rutha the Valkyrie. 'You're raving, my lad! May I remind you that we've got no ship so, unless you can use your magic to make us fly, I don't see how we can leave this island!'

'We shall have another ship tomorrow. My friends are taking care of it. Just trust me!'

'That boy never ceases to amaze me,' said Helmic, happily gnawing a pheasant leg. 'I trust him and I shan't ask any questions! A boy who can shrink a dragon and control wind, fire and water... it's beyond me! He can do anything, can our Amos, even conjure up a ship.'

'Let's finish our meal then and get some sleep,' said Banry. 'We'll see what surprise Amos has in store for us tomorrow.'

'It was Beorf who gave me the idea,' admitted Amos, taking his place by the fire.

'So you said, but what idea? I don't understand,' said Beorf.

Through the night, beyond the sound of the wind whispering in the treetops and the waves breaking on the shore, Amos listened in silence to the songs of the Kelpies. They sang from dusk to dawn. Their voices mingled with the sounds of nature, their long melodious lament spread its soothing effect across the island. The sound of their lullaby, a mixture of wolf howl, whale song and wind song, gently bathed Amos' soul.

The boy had a dream in which he saw a great tower rising to the skies. He also saw his mother, Frilla, at work building the tower. She had aged and her face was more lined, her features etched deeper by physical and mental suffering. She was gaunt and found it hard to breathe.

The dream faded, giving way to an explosion of colours, but Amos' eyes remained closed. He was filled with an indescribable feeling of wellbeing. The magic flowed through him, touching every part of his body while nourishing and invigorating his brain. Hours passed in this way; nothing disturbed his feeling of inner calm – not even the snoring of the Beorites.

Amos had been in a meditation position all night long. When he opened his eyes, he felt as if he had only slept for an hour. Glancing around him he realised that he was no longer touching the ground. He was floating about thirty centimetres above it. He was levitating! But, just as he realised this, Amos fell to the ground and hit his coccyx on a stone. He lay there painfully for a few seconds trying to understand what had happened. The mask-wearer felt rested and relaxed and ready for anything! The night had completely restored his strength.

The Beorites were still fast asleep and snoring so Amos decided to go to the other side of the island by himself. He was eager to see whether the Kelpies had managed to keep their promise.

When he reached the pebbly beach, he could see the ship in the distance. It was ready to go to sea. Tears of joy filled his eyes and he felt choked with a great happiness. The Kelpies were his true friends and the ship looked magnificent!

CHAPTER TEN

THE GREY MAN

The Beorites gawped in amazement! Before them in the morning mist was a magnificent three-masted ship, ten times the size of their burnt-out drakkar. The wreck had been completely renovated from keel to crow's nest. A patchwork of colourful corals filled the holes and the new hull was almost entirely made of shells, sea anemones and starfish. The prow of the ship was decorated with a figurehead of a Kelpie, arms spread wide, head looking straight ahead as if in motion. The deck seemed to sparkle in the sunshine.

Once on board the Beorites were astonished to see that all the rigging was made of plaited seaweed. In the hold they found barrels of drinking water, salt and dried fish, live lobsters and other shellfish all ready for them.

'It's a miracle!' cried Banry, unable to believe his eyes.

'If we'd only known, we could have sunk the drakkar before this!' said Hulot rubbing his chin. 'This ship is just...'

'Extraordinary!' cried Piotr the Giant. 'It's quite simply extraordinary!'

'Do you remember, Amos?' asked Kasso. 'I told you about Skidbladnir before we set off?'

'Yes I remember, the fantastic ship that could travel across land, sea and air.'

'Well,' Kasso continued, 'I've never seen that legendary ship but I'm sure it must be something like this.'

'We do have a problem though,' interrupted Banry. 'There don't seem to be any sails or oars! How are we going to sail it?'

The crew searched all over to find some way of moving the ship. There must be a way of sailing it! It was Goy who spotted two long ropes hanging down into the water at the rear of the ship near the tiller. One was to port and the other to starboard. They reminded him of reins and instinctively, he seized them in both hands. He shook them as if he were driving a chariot and bellowed loudly:

'Forward!'

The ship suddenly pitched forward surrounded by huge waves as twenty-five seahorses popped up alongside the ship. There were twelve on either side with a leader at their head. They were attached to the ship by a complicated system of knots and harnesses. Each one had the head and torso of a thoroughbred horse but from the waist tapered into a long curving tail. The front feet of these aquatic steeds were like large flippers and their skin seemed to be made up of small silver scales.

Thrilled by his discovery, Goy flicked the reins once more and confidently called out: 'Forward, my pretties!'

The seahorses began moving their powerful tails; the ship slowly started to move, gradually picking up speed as it got under way.

'I really like this system!' laughed Piotr the Giant. 'No more exhaustion from rowing or boredom waiting about to catch a favourable wind! I just love this ship... I love it!'

Kasso sat beside his brother and unrolled his precious sea charts. They had not been lost in the fire because the navigator always carried them with him wherever he went.

'Well done, brother,' he said kindly.

'I can't believe I am really driving a team of seahorses!' cried Goy excitedly. 'You can turn the ship easily and we're sailing faster than with a strong wind.'

At the ship's prow Amos filled his lungs with the fresh sea air. Once more he had accomplished the impossible! After they had lost everything, apart from their weapons and a few personal possessions, the Beorites had found another ship, fresh provisions and new hope of reaching Freyja's island. What's more they didn't have to row or wait for a favourable wind. They could all rest as they sailed. The young mask-wearer had done his job well!

All day long the seahorses worked to perfection. They pulled the ship with such steady power that by nightfall Kasso found that they were two days ahead of their original schedule.

Instinctively, without anyone's guidance, the seahorses stopped for the night right in the middle of a field of seaweed where they could feed and rest. The Beorites gathered on the deck to discuss the rest of their journey.

'At this rate we should reach the Great Fog Barrier in less than three days,' declared Kasso.

'All the legends say that it's impossible to cross the barrier!' sighed Hulot. 'Crews get lost in the thick fog and go round and round for months. Sometimes they get shipwrecked on the rocks and end up at the bottom of the sea!'

'There must be some way to get through,' cried Banry. 'We have to get to Freyja's island. The future of our people depends on it!'

'I think I know how we can find our way through,' said Amos. 'From what I understand from the book, Al-Qatrum, I think I can foil the Grey Man. I have a plan!'

Amos explained his plan to his friends who agreed it was worth trying. They continued to talk the plan over while tucking in to some lobsters. Before settling for the night they organised a rota to keep watch. This first night at sea seemed calm and uneventful. As they travelled on towards the Great Fog Barrier, the crew seized the chance to sunbathe, play dice, practice with their weapons and eat.

Goy was thrilled to be able to steer such a wonderful ship and sat in the captain's seat. Thus it was that the Azulson brothers inherited the task of guiding the ship to its destination. Banry was happy to yield his position of authority, putting himself into the hands of his two crewmen. In this way he, too, was able to rest before facing the dangers ahead.

Amos spent hours examining the witch's chest and poring over her spell book. Unfortunately he could find nothing new. Beorf kept a careful eye on the dragon in case it should start to grow. Their luck held and the creature seemed happy to devour the insects the boy gave it. So far all was going well.

One evening, just after the sun had disappeared below the horizon, the ship was suddenly enveloped in a thick mist. Kasso told them that according to his charts, the Great Fog Barrier was not far ahead. Goy slowed the seahorses so that the ship moved cautiously and silently towards its destination. Amos reviewed his plan.

Then he took a deep breath, slipped on his elf-ears and signalled to the crew to stand ready.

The three-masted ship moved slowly onwards for another hour without anything strange or unusual happening. The young mask-wearer was just beginning to wonder whether there was such a creature as the Grey Man when, suddenly, the mist began to move. It billowed up, taking on the appearance of an enormous old man's face. His beard was of bright shimmering mist, but his skin was a tone of deep grey, like a dank, dark autumn morning. Fine droplets of water vapour fell from his mouth as he spoke in a quavering, rasping voice:

'Return from whence you came! You may not enter! Before you is the Great Fog Barrier and I am its keeper. It is written in the laws that govern heaven and hell that no human is allowed to pass beyond this point.'

'Very well,' Amos called to him as he moved to the front of the ship. 'Let me through then!'

'Did you not understand what I just said?' exclaimed the Grey Man.

'Of course I did,' answered Amos brusquely. 'You said that no human may pass through the Great Fog Barrier. But I am no human, I am an elf! Look at my ears!'

The crystal ears, given to him by Gwenfadrilla, had moulded themselves to his, so now Amos had pointed ears and really did look like an elf.

'But… but,' stammered the Grey Man, his misty eyes opening wide, 'elves no longer exist on Earth. They left many centuries ago. How do you explain your presence here? Why do you want to cross the Great Fog Barrier?'

'It's obvious that you haven't left this place for a long time, old man!' spat Amos contemptuously. 'The elves have returned and inhabit several of the world's forests!'

'Well, I didn't know that!' sighed the giant. 'It is true that I've been keeping guard here for a long time and the world changes around me. I have heard no news from the rest of the world for many a year… I am always here in the mist!'

'Let me show you my cargo!' said Amos impatiently. As he spoke the young mask-wearer opened the hatches to reveal a cargo of bears! The Beorites had taken on their animal form. One by one the crewmen clambered out and roamed over the deck.

'An elf travelling with bears? I've never seen the likes of this before,' cried the astonished keeper.

'I am a messenger from the great god Odin,' explained Amos. 'I've got to get to Freyja's island to give her this present.'

'But… I thought Freyja and Odin were at war!' said the misty old giant, puzzled.

'You really are behind with the news! Odin and Freyja are to marry and these bears are a wedding present. You know that they are Odin's favourite creatures. My mission is quite straightforward: deliver the bears to Freyja's island and then go home!'

'Can you guarantee there are no humans on board?' asked the keeper, stunned by Amos' revelations.

'See for yourself!' Amos replied with a weary sigh.

'I'm sure of one thing,' said the keeper as his face slowly disappeared, 'you certainly are an elf – you have all the arrogance and rudeness of your ancestors!'

Amos had played his part well. The mist poured into every corner of the ship. After a short search of the vessel, the keeper's face reappeared in front of them.

'That seems all right. There are no humans on board. You may pass. I wish you a safe journey.'

'Thank you!' cried Amos taking up the seahorses' reins. 'Off we go!'

The ship pitched a little before setting off once more and the Grey Man began to evaporate. As the ship moved onward through the thick fog the Beorites, still on all fours, looked at each other and laughed. Amos had certainly fooled the keeper of the Great Fog Barrier!

From here on the ship was sailing in waters uncharted and unexplored. To the great relief of Amos, Banry and the Azulson brothers, the ship did not fall off the edge of the world and Vidofnir the snake did not devour the crew. The Beorites now had a good ship, full stomachs and great adventures in store. Nothing, it seemed, could stop them!

CHAPTER ELEVEN

THE SEA SERPENTS

The god Loki was boiling with rage and thirsting for revenge. All his plans had failed! Baba Yaga's defeat had filled him with unbearable frustration. His assassin had achieved nothing. How could she have been outsmarted like that? And by two children! He would like to have skinned her alive! He was glad the old hag had roasted! Serve her right!

Things had gone badly for Loki. By destroying the Beorites' drakkar he had planned to kill two birds with one stone: to rid himself of the useless Baba Yaga and to strand the crew to rot on the island. But everything had been ruined by that wretched mask-wearer, Amos Daragon!

Once again, thanks to him, the crew had escaped. Loki had been furious that the Kelpies had come to the rescue of the Beorites. They still had to pass through the

Great Fog Barrier and Loki had thought that would be the end of the expedition, but to his amazement they had got through! Amos had succeeded where the best seamen had failed. He had tricked the world's most vigilant keeper with no trouble at all!

This would not do! Loki, the god of Fire and Discord, could not allow the Beorites to reach Freyja's island. He needed the quarrel between Odin and the goddess of Fertility to continue unabated. He was about to stage something stunning and the possibility of a reconciliation between the gods of Good would threaten his plans.

Loki could not bear being bored and there was nothing that bored him more than days that rolled by peacefully without any trouble. How he hated such days! Before Amos had come on the scene he had often amused himself by playing tricks on the other gods. The dispute between Freyja and Odin that he'd caused had increased his power and he now had some fantastic schemes in mind! He would not let a mere boy, a filthy mask-wearer, destroy his dreams by reconciling his enemies.

Loki would have to act quickly to strike a fatal blow to the expedition. He must wreck the Kelpies' ship, drown the stupid Beorite crew and rid himself, once and for all, of Amos Daragon!

Seated on his heavenly throne, he plucked three hairs from the crown of his head. Stroking them carefully he pronounced these words:

'Three of my hairs become three of my children! Little serpents become great serpents. Do what you must do and do not disappoint me.'

Loki let the three hairs fall from his hand. Landing in the ocean, they turned into three enormous sea serpents about sixty metres long. The creatures' bodies were covered with thick scales and they had huge fangs and flaming eyes. The three sea monsters immediately headed south to find the Beorites.

Loki rubbed his hands together: 'Let's see what you make of that, mask-wearer!'

After a few days the Great Fog Barrier was far behind them. On deck the crew still talked about Amos' trickery. The Beorites, now back in human form, relaxed in the sunshine.

Beorf and Amos had made themselves fishing rods. They had cast their lines at the back of the ship but hadn't yet caught anything.

'As well as being a good magician,' Beorf teased Amos. 'You're a pretty good liar too!'

'More like a good actor, Beorf.' insisted Amos. 'Actually, I didn't really lie, I just tweaked the truth a little.'

The Beorites standing behind them burst out laughing.

'Tweaked the truth! That's a good one!' laughed Helmic.

'Be quiet!' ordered Banry. 'Fetch your weapons, men! I sense trouble!'

'You're right!' said Rutha the Valkyrie. 'The air feels heavy… I can smell death everywhere.'

'There! Behind us!' cried Piotr the Giant. 'Full speed ahead, Goy! Fast as you can!'

Goy shook the reins and the seahorses seemed to become jet-propelled. Three shadows, just visible in the water, were fast approaching the ship.

'What is it?' asked Amos anxiously.

'Sea serpents!' answered Helmic, gritting his teeth. 'I've fought them before, but never three at once! It's not going to be easy.'

'You mean it's impossible!' cried Hulot.

'Remember,' said Banry, gripping his axe tightly. 'You have to put their eyes out! It's the only way to beat them. Come on then. Who's going to dive first?'

'Me!' cried Piotr climbing up the mast. 'You keep them busy and I'll deal with the first one.'

Kasso took his bow and arrows and stood next to his brother at the prow of the ship. It was clear that the seahorses could not outrun their pursuers. The serpents dived and suddenly surfaced under the ship, hitting the hull hard. The ship reeled and they all lost their balance.

A serpent's head emerged on the port side, swallowing one of the seahorses. The creature struggled and whinnied in terror. The sight horrified Amos and Beorf's blood froze.

A second head appeared near the back of the ship. As the serpent opened its mouth to lunge at the hull, Kasso fired an arrow that stuck in the back of its throat making it lose a little ground.

Directly in front of them the third serpent sprang up, cutting right across the ship's path. Skilfully, Goy managed to steer round it, skimming the monster's flank.

Just at that moment a terrible war cry rang out as Piotr the Giant, half man, half bear, leapt down from the mast top and landed on a serpent's head. The Beorite held a long knife between his teeth and plunged his claws into the creature's skin to give himself some grip. The monster dived, taking Piotr down with him into the depths of the ocean.

As Amos watched another seahorse was swallowed and behind the ship the serpent with Kasso's arrow in its throat returned to the attack.

Helmic was ready. He'd had time to prepare a makeshift grappling hook and rope. He spun it round his head and hurled it at the serpent, managing to wrap it round the creature's neck. The crew all took hold of the rope and pulled hard. The serpent's head crashed onto the deck, smashing part of the rail.

Banry leapt on the creature, swung his axe in the air and brought it down between the monster's eyes. Black sticky blood poured over the deck. Rutha the Valkyrie put out the creature's right eye with a skilful thrust of her spear. Pain only increased the serpent's strength and it swung its head, tearing out the rear mast and throwing Aldred into the sea. It then grabbed Helmic in its teeth and flung him backwards, a good twenty metres.

Banry yelled at the top of his voice: 'Two bears overboard! Two bears overboard!'

Amos had to do something. The mask-wearer seized a spear and concentrating for a few seconds, he called up his air magic. He threw his spear at the half-blinded monster. The wind carried it with astonishing speed and it sank deep into the serpent's throat.

Beorf called, 'Good shot, Amos! It's my turn now. Here's one who won't be eating any more seahorses!'

Following Piotr's example, Beorf flung himself on to the head of the serpent on the port side. The creature swung its head round and flung the boy back onto the deck. Beorf let out a long howl as he flew through the air, and landed in the opening to the hold. He rolled down the steps – head first into a barrel of salt cod!

Goy still held the reins but with three seahorses missing on the port side it was becoming difficult to steer the ship.

On the poop deck Banry, Kasso and Rutha quickly

weighed up the situation: 'their' serpent, mortally wounded by Amos' spear, was about to die. Kasso was firing arrows furiously, aiming at the creature's good eye. With Helmic, Piotr and Aldred overboard they had better finish the battle as quickly as possible!

Piotr, still clinging to 'his' serpent, was nowhere to be seen, and neither was Hulot.

The young mask-wearer found himself face to face with the serpent that had just flung Beorf into the hold. The creature lashed out and grabbed him in its terrible jaws! Amos was in danger of being crushed to death.

Knowing the pain that toothache can inflict, he seized hold of one of the serpent's teeth and directed his fire magic to his hands. Instantly the monster opened its jaws, howling with pain as the nerve in its tooth began to fry.

Amos fell hard on to the ship's deck. Apart from a few grazes he was unhurt. The brief spell in the monster's jaws reminded him that, despite his powers, a mask-wearer is not invincible. Amos knew how lucky he had been to get off so lightly.

But, with renewed fury, the beast turned on him again. Twice he dodged the snapping jaws. As it came at him a third time Amos opened his mouth and, like a dragon, aimed a burst of flame at the creature's head. This new form of attack caused the serpent to draw back in surprise.

Then Amos remembered Sartigan's words. The old man always said it was pointless to use your muscles when faced with an enemy larger and stronger than you. First and foremost you must fight with your brain. To illustrate his point, he had shown Amos how a tiny, fragile bubble could travel through water.

'A bubble!' thought Amos. 'That's what I need!'

When the serpent attacked yet again, jaws wide open to bite, the mask-wearer grabbed a dagger and scratched its lower lip. The monster drew back and then suddenly began to shake its head from side to side. Using his powers, Amos had aimed a tiny bubble of air towards the creature's cut so that it would enter its bloodstream. He knew that the consequences of air getting into the bloodstream could be disastrous! The mask-wearer increased the size of his bubble and waited a few seconds. The bubble passed right through the monster's body until it reached its brain. The sea serpent shuddered violently, then dropped dead on the fore deck. Its body slithered off the ship and sank slowly into the ocean.

The Beorites at the back of the ship had also got the better of 'their' serpent. As Banry and Rutha, splattered with blood, threw its remains overboard Kasso shouted:

'Turn the ship round, Goy! We've lost Aldred, Helmic and Piotr overboard. We've got to find them!'

'Give me a moment,' answered Goy. 'I'm missing

three seahorses on the port side! I'll have to even them up.'

'We've no time for that!' yelled Banry. 'Just do your best to get us back!'

'I'm doing all I can!' groaned Goy, but his arms were numb with exhaustion. Slowly, and with great difficulty he turned the ship round.

'Hulot! We've lost Hulot, too!' cried Rutha.

'No, I'm here!' answered the Beorite climbing up from the hold. 'When I saw the serpents attacking the ship I thought it would be best to go below and check for any damage. So I did! Everything is fine!'

'Coward!' spat Rutha.

'Me, a coward?' cried Hulot indignantly. 'I'm no coward, I'm just careful! I'm not a coward.'

Beorf, still dazed and covered with salt cod, also emerged from the hold.

'Have we won?' he asked, staggering a little.

'Yes,' Amos told him. 'But we've lost Helmic, Aldred and Piotr.'

'No!' exclaimed Beorf. 'When I last saw Piotr he was hanging on to a serpent's head.'

'I'm afraid Aldred and Helmic went overboard and we're trying to find them,' said Banry.

The Beorites searched for hours without finding the missing crewmen. The sea was calm and the ship moved slowly, leaving a winding wake behind it.

The seahorses were exhausted. Shattered by their encounter with the sea serpents they finally halted in the middle of a vast field of seaweed. There was nothing for it. The ship could not move another inch before sunrise.

'What shall we do now,' asked Goy.

'We'll have to keep scanning the horizon till nightfall,' said Banry dejectedly. 'Then we'll light a fire in a brazier on deck so that our friends might see us and swim towards us... if they still have the strength, that is!'

Kasso lit a fire as Banry had ordered and the anxious, exhausted Beorites tried their best to get some sleep. Amos and Beorf were on the first watch. The two boys sat side by side gazing at the stars.

'Do you know something, Amos? This is just how I felt when my parents died. The pain is just the same. Do you know what I mean? There's a sort of empty place inside me, a hole that's impossible to fill. I feel as though my soul is just waiting to slip through it to go and join them.'

'Yes,' answered Amos. 'I know what you mean. I felt the same when my father died. And when Medusa looked in the mirror and turned to dust. It was such a shock!'

'I often think about her. I can't get her out of my head. It's as if her image was imprinted on me once I'd looked into her eyes. I sometimes dream about her and all I see is her face. Do you remember it?'

'Of course I do! She was so gentle and had such a pretty smile.'

'That's a good description! Still… it was a bit strange to have snakes instead of hair, don't you think?'

'Well, if you really want to know… a boy who can turn himself into a bear is quite unusual too, if you ask me!'

'I suppose so,' yawned Beorf, 'but everyone has something a little special that makes them stand out from the rest. Oh look, Amos… a falling star!'

'Make a wish, my friend!'

'I wish I could see Medusa again,' said the young Beorite spontaneously.

The boys fell silent in the moonlight.

CHAPTER TWELVE

LOST AT SEA

At first light Goy woke the rest of the crew in a complete panic:

'The seahorses! Our seahorses have gone!'

'What are you saying?' demanded Banry, opening his eyes with some difficulty.

'I couldn't sleep so I decided to try and even up the seahorses' harness. I climbed down the rope ladder and that's when I saw we had no seahorses. Not a single one!'

'We're in a fine mess now, then!' sighed Rutha who'd heard him.

Banry went to see for himself if Goy was right. It was true, the seahorses had slipped their harness and gone. Without them the ship could not move. What were they to do?

Even Amos' powers over water, air and fire were no

use in their present situation. He could not yet create enough wind to move a ship.

The boy tried to summon the Kelpies once more. This time, however, his message did not reach them.

'We're stuck here then!' said Banry, sounding desperate.

'What are we going to do?' asked Hulot anxiously. 'Our supplies are running down and we'll soon be out of drinking water.'

'I really don't know!' confessed Banry, crestfallen. 'Does anyone have an idea? Can your magic help us at all, Amos?'

'I don't think so,' replied the mask-wearer. 'I've been wracking my brains but I can't think how to get us out of this! My powers are still limited. I've tried getting the salt out of seawater so we can drink it but I still haven't had any luck! If I had more power stones for the Mask of Water then I'm sure I could do it.'

'So we just have to hope for a miracle!' exclaimed Hulot, panic-stricken.

'I'm sure something will turn up,' Banry tried to reassure him. 'We've been through worse, haven't we? Since we set off we've met a witch, hordes of spiders and sea serpents. All that on top of the Grey Man and our drakkar going up in flames! We have lost our friends and now here we are prisoners on a ship in the middle of the ocean. There's no way to escape so we might as well save our strength, our saliva and keep out of the sun. That's my advice.'

'Let's go down into the hold,' suggested Rutha, gathering her things. 'At least we'll be in the shade.'

'I wish I could tell you that there's an island nearby,' added Kasso. 'But I don't have any charts for this ocean.'

'This is dire!' sighed Goy. 'I was enjoying sailing this ship. Now we're stuck here!'

The crew settled down in the hold and the waiting began. Every hour Banry went out to scan the horizon. He was looking for an island, a big coral reef or somewhere else they could land. Nothing. Hours and hours went by, but still there was nothing.

A week later nothing had changed. Kasso could tell from the stars that the ship had not shifted an inch. Ocean currents usually carry a ship along. All sorts of floating objects large and small normally drift with the waves and the wind. But the Kelpies' ship did not move. It seemed as though a huge anchor was holding them prisoner. Goy and Banry had already dived under the ship to see if something was preventing it moving, but there was nothing.

'It seems the gods are against us!' declared Banry.

'We must be the playthings of some god who wants us to die,' added Kasso. 'There's no way out for us. This ship will be our tomb!'

'I knew I should have stayed in Upsgran,' mumbled Hulot. 'I shall never see my vegetable patch or my flowers ever again. It will be written in legend that Hulot Hulson, who once slew a dragon with a single blow of his sword, died miserably at sea.'

'We must be victims of another of Loki's plots,' sighed Rutha, 'unless we can fly out of here we are doomed.'

'Unless we can fly!' cried Amos. 'Why didn't I think of that before?'

The boy ran to the witch's chest and opened it:

'Right, I'll explain as best I can. First of all, in this chest there are all sorts of potions, powders, oils and strange mixtures. I don't know how to use them, of course, but I can probably find out from the spell book. I proved that by shrinking the dragon and there he is, still in his jar. Baba Yaga must have used a spell from her notebook to turn herself into a crow.'

'We're with you so far...' said Banry. 'Go on!'

'This phial seems to hold a transforming elixir. There are only about two mouthfuls left. I'm going to shrink the witch's chest. Then I'll turn Beorf and I into crows. You must fasten the chest round my neck and we'll fly off to find Freyja's island. Once there we'll find help and come back. It's the only way!'

'It's better to give it a try than just waiting to die of hunger and thirst on the ship,' replied Banry.

'We may die anyway,' added Rutha, 'but at least we'll die with hope in our hearts. True warriors don't give up, they live on hope.'

Hulot and the Azulson brothers agreed.

'In that case let's not waste any more time!' said Amos opening the book. 'Right, Beorf, I'll start with you. Take this phial and swallow one mouthful…no more! Oh yes, put the dragon in the chest first. We'll take it with us as it's our responsibility. We can put our own things in there as well.'

Beorf stepped forward and took the phial. He sniffed it and pulled a face.

'It smells disgusting. Like sheep droppings mixed with rotten eggs!'

'You have to do it Beorf, it's our only hope.'

'I'll do it,' he agreed and pinched his nose. 'And don't worry, I'll only drink one mouthful!'

Beorf swallowed the potion and gave a violent shudder of disgust. Amos looked at the book and said in a loud clear voice:

'Vaslimas mas crow, mas mas koite, valimas y jul!'

Beorf's body began to jerk, then he fell to the ground, metamorphosing into a crow as he did so. The bird had fur on its legs and a bear's fur all over its body. Only its wings had feathers. Amos thought that this must be because his friend was a Beorite and the potion had been devised for a human. He memorized a few spells before putting the notebook into the chest. As he sprinkled a white powder over it he said:

'Aton na bar ouf, oug ignakar kilk!'

The chest shrank to the size of a pendant. Amos quickly swallowed the last mouthful from the little phial and repeated the words:

'Vaslimas mas crow, mas mas koite, valimas y jul!'

His body quickly changed into that of a bird. It was very painful, it felt as if all his bones were breaking into a thousand fragments. A dreadful heat went through him as his nose turned into a beak and his skull reshaped itself. The Beorites fastened the pendant around his neck then proceeded to carry their two feathered friends up onto the deck. Goy held Amos and Banry carried Beorf, who was croaking in panic. He was trying to tell the Beorites:

'Don't throw me up into the air! I don't know how to fly! I need to get used to my wings. Don't throw me yet!'

Only Amos could understand what he was trying to say. He told him:

'Spread your wings, Beorf. It'll be all right!'

'It'll be all right will it?' said Beorf agitatedly. 'You've got feathers and I've got fur! How many furry creatures do you know that can fly?'

'Your wings are made of feathers,' Amos tried to

reassure his friend. 'You've just got to beat your arms... I mean your wings!'

Solemnly the Beorites walked to the front of the ship, and threw the two birds over the rail. Amos spread his wings and began to flap vigorously. He felt the air supporting him and realised he did not need to wear himself out to keep his position. It was just a question of balance.

Beorf, on the other hand, spread his wings and glided a few metres before plunging head first into the sea. He had to work twice as hard to try to recover from this bad start. By flapping his wings furiously he eventually managed to get free of the water. The Beorites shouted words of encouragement from the ship. They applauded wildly when the furry crow finally took off from the water to climb slowly up into the sky. Amos glided down to meet his friend.

'Are you all right, Beorf?' croaked the mask-wearer.

'Oh yes, the water's fine!'

'Did you forget that we are birds and not fish?' mocked Amos.

'Very funny I'm sure!' replied Beorf, somewhat irritated.

'Come on, Beorf, let's fly higher and see if we can see any islands.'

'You lead the way and I'll follow.'

The two crows climbed right up to the clouds.

'Look!' cried Beorf. 'I can see something over there!'

'Where?' asked Amos looking down.

'No. Not in the sea! There, in front!'

'Oh no, no....'

'What is it?' asked Beorf who couldn't quite make out what the flying creature could be. 'It's heading straight for us, I think!'

'Someone really is out to get us! That, dear Beorf, is a griffon.'

'What's a griffon?'

'I remember reading about it in Al-Qatrum. It's like a lion crossed with an eagle. Its back end has a long tail and it has sharp claws on its feet, but at the front it has the body, wings, head and talons of an eagle. It's incredibly strong and can lift a horse off its feet. It lives in mountains, caves and on cliffs.'

'That must mean we're not far from land!'

'We've got to deal with that thing first. It's heading straight for us and I think it sees us as breakfast!'

'That's strange, I thought that griffons were friendly creatures,' said Beorf, flying as fast as he could.

'That's just fairy stories! But you'll soon find out for yourself just how nice they are. Look out! Here it comes!'

The griffon gave a piercing cry that sent a shiver through the boys. It was slightly bigger than a horse yet it flew with the agility of a bird of prey. It was an awesome sight. It had dark blue feathers at the back of its neck, its body was black with a red breast and it had huge white wings. It had long pointed ears rather like a donkey's. A thick golden pelt covered the back of its body.

'You asked me about furry animals that could fly... well here's one for a start. Shall I introduce you?'

'No thanks,' yelled Beorf. 'It's kind of you, but I don't need friends like him!'

The griffon flew just above Beorf, trying to grab him in its beak. The Beorite plunged towards the sea to avoid its deadly attack.

Thwarted, the creature swooped on Amos, grasping him with its right talons. The boy felt an enormous pressure, making it hard for him to breathe. Seeing what had happened, Beorf dived at the griffon and dug his beak into the back of its head. This only maddened the creature, which turned to grab him with its other talons. Now Beorf was a prisoner too.

'What can we do?' croaked Beorf, looking at Amos.

'I... I... don't know,' gasped the mask-wearer. 'I think he's taking us back to his lair... to eat!'

'Have you got any plan?'

'I'm thinking... really hard!'

CHAPTER THIRTEEN

THE GRIFFON'S LAIR

The griffon carried Amos and Beorf in its talons for a good while before they caught sight of a little island far below. The tiny dot of land, floating in the ocean like a cork, had steep reddish cliffs. It was a bird's paradise. Thousands and thousands of birds criss-crossed the air, fishing in the sea and nesting in the cliffs' rocky faces. There was a plateau in the centre of the island, covered with bright green grass, in the middle of which Amos could see a circle of standing stones. Dozens of wild horses were galloping about.

'This must be it,' thought Amos. 'It must be Freyja's island. This griffon must be its guardian. With a herd of horses for food, thousands of birds for company, it's an ideal spot to keep a look out for strangers.'

As the griffon swooped in with its prisoners all the birds flew off, leaving the way clear. It flew right up to the cliff and into a hole. This was its cave, its lair!

The creature tossed the two crows into the back of the cave and licked its chops. Amos and Beorf landed head first on a pile of horse bones.

'Quick Amos, we need a plan,' gasped Beorf.

'We need to take it by surprise!' said Amos and muttered an incomprehensible spell from the witch's notebook twice over. The griffon was startled to see its prey suddenly turn into two boys and backed away in surprise. Then it let out an angry cry and prepared to fight.

'Well done, Amos!' cried Beorf, admiringly. 'Do we attack?'

'No,' replied the mask-wearer, 'I thought we should give our young dragon some exercise! Get ready to smash the jar!'

Amos removed his pendant and uttered another spell. Instantly the chest returned to its normal size. Beorf grabbed the glass jar that held the dragon and threw it to the ground. The container smashed and the mask-wearer repeated the last spell once more.

The griffon watched in astonishment as a furious young dragon appeared. The two creatures eyed each other savagely. In spite of its size the griffon was not sure if it could win the fight. Even a new-born dragon is incredibly powerful and filled with rage. They know no fear and have a deadly killer instinct.

The dragon struck first. With one bound it threw

itself at the griffon, biting it hard in the shoulder. Scarlet blood spurted from the griffon's wound. It retaliated, using its leonine back legs to tear bits of scaly armour from the young dragon's abdomen. The dragon gave a scream of rage and seized the griffon by the throat. The winged beast's talons dug deeply into the dragon's wound, trying to reach its heart.

Motionless, Amos and Beorf watched the spectacle. With their backs to the cave wall and standing on the bed of horse bones they awaited the outcome. The young mask-wearer could intervene by using his magic, but in whose favour? It seemed obvious that the victor would turn on him and Beorf next. The wisest course was just to wait and see. In any case there was no shrinking powder left. He would need another way to get rid of the winner.

The two combatants continued biting and tearing at each other with their claws.

'They'll kill each other,' cried Beorf. 'It's horrible!'

'I don't know how this will turn out, Beorf,' said Amos. 'If we have to fight my magic is ready! Wait for my signal won't you?'

'That's for sure,' said Beorf. 'I've no wish to be roasted by one of your fire balls.'

The two beasts were beginning to tire. They were both bleeding profusely and it was impossible to tell which one would overcome the other. They struck, bit and clawed one another viciously. Cries of rage and dreadful groans filled the cave.

Suddenly the little dragon, with a final supreme effort, lunged at its rival, stabbing it in the side with its pointed tail. The griffon staggered backwards and sank to the ground. Its lungs were ruptured.

The griffon groaned as it lay coughing on the ground. Then it closed its eyes and died with one last spine-chilling squawk.

The dragon was so horribly wounded that it didn't even notice the boys, but curled up in a ball on top of the pile of bones. It licked its wounds carefully then fell into a deep sleep. It had had enough!

'What shall we do now?' whispered Beorf anxious not to wake it.

'Let's go to the entrance,' said Amos, signalling to his friend to make as little noise as possible.

The dragon began to snore. In truth the two boys could actually have shouted, sung loud songs or even thrown stones at it without disturbing it. The dragon was hovering between life and death. It was very badly wounded and was still too young to heal itself. Its life was draining away.

Beorf and Amos stood at the cave entrance planning what they should do. The cave was hewn out of the cliff face. The sea was a hundred metres below them, but it was a sixty-metre climb up to the island's grassy plateau.

'It's a pity we're no longer birds!' cried Beorf. 'Is there none of that disgusting potion left?'

'I thought you'd get to like it!' laughed Amos. 'I don't think we've got any choice. Either we jump or we climb!'

'Let's climb,' decided Beorf rubbing his hands. 'My claws should be really useful.'

The Beorite took off his shoes, tied the laces together and slung them round his neck. His hands and feet were now bear's paws and he began to climb the cliff face. Clinging on to the rock he called to Amos:

'Follow my footsteps and place your hands and feet exactly where I do. I'll try to find the easiest way up for you. If you lose your balance, grab hold of my leg. My claws give me a good grip and you won't drag me down.'

'You're in charge this time! Just be careful, Beorf.'

The first part of the climb was fairly straightforward. Beorf chose the easiest route with the best footholds. The boys climbed slowly, with the manimal clinging firmly to the rock face, always making sure he had a good firm foothold.

Amos had great difficulty keeping up with his friend. He forced himself to concentrate on what he was doing and tried hard not to look down, but it wasn't easy. With each new foothold he glimpsed the waves crashing on the rocks below and felt dizzy. He was not as strong as Beorf and his arms and legs were tiring. Amos realised he would never reach the top.

'I can't climb any further, Beorf!' he called up. 'My hands are shaking and my legs have turned to jelly. We've hardly gone ten metres and I can't go any further. I'm going down! I'll find some other way.'

'No! You can't! This cliff face is very dangerous to climb but you won't survive if you try to go down. If you lose your footing you'll fall and smash onto the rocks.

'Well I'm in a real mess then!' mumbled Amos. 'You'll need to come up with a plan this time!'

'Grab hold of my leg and climb onto my back. I'm strong enough to carry you!'

'That's completely mad! You can't climb up with my weight!'

'Never underestimate the strength of a Beorite, Amos,' declared Beorf confidently. 'Come on! Up you come!'

With difficulty, Amos grasped hold of his friend's leg and slowly hauled himself up onto his back. A strong wind was blowing which almost ended this hazardous manoeuvre. The extra weight on Beorf's shoulders made him recall one of Sartigan's stories. It was about true friends, bound together to share the same fate:

'There was once a lonely frog who met a very nice mouse. They chatted for some time and decided to meet up again the next day. They met again the following day and every day after that. As they were now such good friends, the frog suggested that they should never part.

He held up a piece of string and asked the mouse to tie it round his leg. The frog would do likewise so that they would always be together and never leave each other's side. The mouse agreed.

'A hungry rook that was flying by spotted the juicy frog and snapped it up. The mouse, still attached by the string was carried off at the same time and both friends ended their life in the rook's stomach.'

Sartigan had said the story was about recognising how far you were ready to go to share a friend's fate before it became wiser to sever the bonds of friendship.

Beorf knew he was endangering his own life to save his friend.

Thinking of Sartigan's story he asked himself: 'Am I ready to die here with Amos?' Without any hesitation the answer was 'Yes'. The ties that bound these two boys together were, by now, stronger than death itself.

Beorf gritted his teeth and climbed with renewed strength and energy for the next few metres before stopping to get his breath back.

Amos asked him: 'Did Sartigan ever tell you the story about the frog and the mouse?'

'Yes, I know that one,' answered Beorf breathing heavily. 'Why do you ask?'

'If I think that you can't do this, Beorf, I will throw myself down there!' Amos told him solemnly. 'I won't be like the frog and drag you to your death with me.'

'I understand' said Beorf, panting. 'But you must …
let me… show you… that I can save your life too! You
saved me from the cage in Great Bratel. I owe you!
Hang on tight now… We're off again!'

Beorf no longer had any doubts. He found enough
inner strength and skill to climb the rest of the cliff. His
feet followed his hands in perfect coordination. He kept
control of his breathing, his body and his feelings. He
would succeed!

The two boys reached the cliff top safely and Beorf
lay breathless on his back in the long grass. His heart
was pounding furiously. His arms and legs felt as weak
as a kitten's. As he watched the clouds overhead, he
smiled and said:

'You're heavy, Amos. Perhaps you should go on a
diet!'

'You're right!' he answered, laughing. 'But save your
breath and have a rest. You deserve it for once!'

'If I wasn't so shattered,' Beorf teased, 'I would give
you a good hiding for that!'

'You Beorites are so aggressive!' laughed Amos. 'Real
animals!'

The two boys laughed loudly together.

CHAPTER FOURTEEN

THE FINAL JOURNEY

Banry, Rutha, Hulot and the Azulson brothers had watched the two crows fly away from the ship. They saw them soar upwards until they disappeared among the clouds. Just as they were about to go back down to the hold, they saw a wolf sitting calmly on the prow of the ship. It had its back to them and was staring towards the horizon. The startled crew drew their swords and seized their battle-axes. The wolf turned to face them and spoke in a low melodious voice:

'Put those away. Your weapons cannot hurt me, I am immortal.'

'A talking wolf,' exclaimed Hulot in surprise. 'Well, I never…!'

'What's that? You think wolves can't talk!' mocked the wolf. 'I've never heard that before! You must be as stupid as you look. It's easy to see that your stomach is far more developed than your brain.'

'Who are you and what do you want?' demanded Banry, stepping forwards.

'Ah, you must be Banry, the fearless warrior!' declared the wolf. 'The chieftain who steps forward to protect his people! What a fine picture of selfless devotion!'

'You haven't answered my question,' repeated Banry. 'Who are you?'

'I am the avatar of the god Loki,' announced the creature with a slight bow.

'The what of who?' said Goy, scratching his head.

'Let me explain,' the creature continued, 'I am a messenger from the god Loki. I am his ambassador or, if you prefer, his representative on earth. Is that better, my dear Goy, or would you like me to repeat all that in words of less than three syllables? Loki is a god, a very important god and he speaks through me.'

'And what does Loki want?' snapped Banry. 'What does the vilest, the least intelligent of the gods want from us? To what do we owe the honour of your wretched visit? Have you come to make trouble? Are you recruiting disciples for Loki? Speak before my mortal hands seize your immortal neck to turn you into a piece of fur!'

'I can see you are a true son of Odin!' cried the wolf

with a half smile. 'I've come to make a bargain with you. I will free you from your present difficulties, you can go home and this little adventure can be forgotten! For your part, you must vow never again to try to reach Freyja's island! What do you think?'

The Beorites looked at each other knowingly. The wolf had just confirmed their suspicions. It was all too obvious! Their problems, the witch, the burning of their drakkar, the sea serpents and now their imprisonment in mid-ocean were all the work of Loki. He was behind everything!

'And why should we accept your proposal?' asked Rutha, suspiciously.

'To save your lives,' answered the wolf calmly. 'It's the only way you will survive this adventure. If you accept, you will see your village and families once more and can return to your old way of life. If you refuse, I shall sink the ship! You Beorites may be good swimmers but you are too far from land to reach the shore! Loki was greatly surprised that you managed to destroy his three sea serpents.'

'We are sons of Odin!' declared Goy.

'We fear no danger or adversary!' Kasso added proudly.

The wolf strolled around them. 'You Beorites are blinded by your courage. Your race will soon cease to exist, that is inevitable! You are too stupid to survive.'

'You can do what you like to us,' said Banry haughtily. 'But we Beorites have other means of survival.'

'I suppose you mean Amos Daragon and his faithful friend Beorf Bromanson?' sneered the wolf.

A heavy silence fell over the ship.

'As I speak, they are already dead…' the wolf went on. 'I do not know what magic or potions they used to turn themselves into crows, but Loki found out. They were both devoured as soon as they landed on Freyja's island before they had a chance to reach their goal. Such a pity isn't? The island is guarded by a ferocious griffon and Loki gave it the task of dealing with them. So there is no further hope for the Beorites or this ship. You mere mortals should never try to play games with the gods. Now… does my proposal interest you more?'

'You are lying!' cried Banry. 'Amos is more clever than Loki and Beorf has the courage of the Bromansons – he is descended from the first man-bear that Odin created. His blood is pure and his name is great, they will not fail.'

'Shut your filthy mouth and sink our ship!' yelled Hulot. 'All my life I have been afraid: afraid of pain, afraid of dying and afraid of adventure. I am no thoroughbred! But today I have found out what I am – a true Beorite. We Beorites never surrender! We cannot be bought and we have no respect for those who despise us. We have fought together and we will die together!'

'I think you have your answer,' said Banry simply. 'We will not go home with our tails between our legs. Neither will we live with defeat and regret. We began this journey for one reason only: to speak to Freyja, queen of earth and heaven, to ask her to lift the curse that afflicts our race. We want to plead our cause and ask her for mercy. We have overcome all of Loki's obstacles so far and we are not afraid… even of death itself!'

'It would have been so much simpler if you had just stayed quietly at home,' sighed the wolf.

'You were told to be quiet,' continued Banry. 'We don't wish to hear another word from your foul mouth: we will die with our ears unsullied. Do what you will and clear off!'

Each of the crew placed their right hand on their heart. Together and in one voice they recited these words:

Thanks be to Odin for our sorrows and our joys
Thanks for our sweat and the fruits of our labour
We give thanks for brave enemies and faithful friends
Save for us a seat at your table
We shall dine together tonight!

The Beorites then formed a circle on deck to thank one another for their friendship and loyalty. Together they raised their arms to heaven and gave such a war cry that both the sky and the sea trembled. This was their way of telling Odin that they were about to arrive in Åsgard.

The wolf disappeared and the ship sank, carrying the Beorites with it into the depths of the ocean.

CHAPTER FIFTEEN

THE QUEEN RETURNS

The villagers of Upsgran could not believe their eyes. A delegation of forty warriors had just arrived in the main square. Their heads were shaven and their skin, as dark as night, was decorated with wonderful, brightly coloured war paint. Each was adorned with heavy jewellery made of gold and precious stones, some wore bone jewellery through their nose and ears, too. They wore feathers and exotic animal skins the likes of which the Beorites had never seen before.

A beautiful young girl with skin the colour of ebony emerged from the centre of the group. She was barely eleven years old yet she looked astonishingly regal. Her hair was piled high at the back of her head and wrapped around her like a sari was a magnificent crimson robe. She seemed covered in ornate gold jewellery: necklaces, rings, bracelets and many fine amulets, large and small.

She bowed politely to those who had gathered round and spoke in perfect Nordic: 'Good morning! My name is Lolya and I am looking for two friends called Amos Daragon and Beorf Bromanson. Have they been here? Please tell me, it is extremely urgent.'

'Well… er…,' stammered the fat innkeeper's wife. 'We do indeed know them. They lived here with us for a few months but they went to sea weeks ago and we don't know when they will be back.'

'You don't know? You really have no idea when they will return?' asked the girl looking distressed.

'No, I'm sorry. They set off for Freyja's island to sort out… well, let's just say for an important mission that could save our village. But why do you want to see them?'

'I came to join them,' declared Lolya. 'Some time ago the three of us had a strange adventure and Amos saved my life. I returned to my own distant country quite certain that our time together was over. I am queen of the Morgorian tribe and I assumed I would spend my life peacefully in the service of my people. I thought that I was going home to my own land and my own people to rule them faithfully until I died.'

'So, what happened then?' asked an old Beorite at the back of the crowd who dearly loved stories.

'I began to see visions,' she continued. 'Horrible images of myself shrivelled up and mummified alive! I saw that my people were going to kill me. They insulted me, saying that I had not followed my heart. I realised that I was not meant to spend my life ruling the Morgorians, but to help Amos Daragon fulfil his destiny. I have a talent, a knowledge that I must use to serve Amos. And then there was a message.'

The innkeeper's wife interrupted Lolya: 'Let's all go to the inn. We can hear the rest of your story there while we eat and drink. What do you think, young Loya?'

'Lolya,' the girl corrected her. 'Of course, but first I must dismiss my escort.'

The young queen uttered a few words to the exotic Morgorians who put down Lolya's belongings, turned and disappeared into the forest.

'They could have stayed,' said the innkeeper's wife, somewhat disappointed. 'They were invited too!'

'It's for the best,' answered Lolya. 'I no longer rule the Morgorians and have passed all my powers and privileges to my younger sister. Our kingdom will need to rebuild itself and those men are its most valiant warriors. They are anxious to return home to take up their duties and to protect my sister, the new queen. They wanted to leave as quickly as possible and I've given them leave to go.'

The whole village piled into the inn. Things had been getting interesting in Upsgran recently and the villagers were enjoying it. Lolya continued her story:

'I was telling you about the message…'

'Go on,' said the innkeeper's wife, licking her lips. 'A mysterious message you said.'

'I had a dream about Frilla, Amos' mother.'

A hushed silence fell over the listeners. Even the flies ceased buzzing. The woman asked:

'Did you know that his mother was taken away by the Red Caps, a race of vicious, war-like goblins? They say she was sold into slavery!'

'Yes, that's what she told me in my dream. She also told me where she was being held captive. It's a place called the tower of El-Bab. She is enslaved there, helping to build the world's highest tower. She also told me about a man called Sartigan.'

'Sartigan!' everyone said at once.

'We know him, too,' said the woman. 'He is Amos' and Beorf's teacher. He's a strange fellow, always wears an orange robe and he has a very long beard. He wears it wrapped around his neck like a scarf.'

'Well,' said Lolya. 'He has also been taken prisoner and works as a slave. In my dream, Frilla told me that Sartigan had set out to find her. He kept his plan to himself once Amos had decided to go to Freyja's island. Sartigan did not want to distract him by giving him false hope. It was also an ideal opportunity for the old teacher to see how the eastern slave markets operated. But luck was not with him and he was captured. This is why I have left my people. It is the reason I have decided to join Amos in his quest as mask-wearer. I know I can help him and I am at his service.'

'Well,' said the innkeeper's wife. 'Old Sartigan really is in a mess! But sadly, we have no way of contacting Amos. You'll have to be patient.'

'May I stay in Sartigan's house while I wait for Amos to come back?' asked Lolya.

'I don't think he would mind,' said the woman.

Lolya thanked the Beorites. Some of the villagers guided her through the forest and helped carry her belongings to Sartigan's house, where they left her.

It was a simple little cabin with whitewashed walls. Inside and out it was spotlessly clean. There was little furniture, just a few rugs on the wooden floor, a big fireplace and dozens of jars of tea. Lolya took some candles out of her bag and placed them in a circle on the floor. Then she removed all her jewellery and amulets and stepped into the middle of the circle. The girl uttered some words and then danced a slow ritual dance for a few minutes.

Lolya had not told the Beorites that she had seen the birth of a dragon in her dream. She also knew that the creature was in danger and was close to death. It was vital that Amos should bring it back with him. She felt absolutely certain that the dragon would play an important role in Amos' quest to re-establish balance in the world. It must not be allowed to die! The mask-wearer had to tend its wounds and bring it back to Upsgran. The young queen knew that nothing came down to chance in this life. Amos' fate depended, in some inexplicable way, on this dragon. Sometime in the future his fate would be linked to this wounded creature.

Lolya performed her ritual once an hour for the next three days.

CHAPTER SIXTEEN

FREYJA

After resting for a while Amos and Beorf walked towards the centre of the island.

'When the griffon had us in its talons, I spotted some ancient raised tombs over that way,' said Amos.

'How do you set about talking to a goddess?' asked Beorf, distractedly.

'That's a good question... I haven't the faintest idea.'

'Ok,' sighed the manimal. 'I suppose we'll make it up as we go along, as usual!'

After walking for about an hour they could see in the distance the tombs that Amos had seen from the air.

Suddenly, twelve women appeared. They had snow-white skins, crimson lips and eyes with a faint blue sparkle. Their thick blonde hair was braided into two plaits hanging down to the waist and they were draped in a fine, gauze-like material that fluttered as they moved.

These were the Brising who guarded Freyja's necklace. The twelve women spoke in unison:

'We are happy to see you, Amos Daragon and Beorf Bromanson. Our Ramusberget sisters have told us all about you. We welcome you to Freyja's island.'

'Thank you,' replied Amos politely, nodding his head in greeting. 'It was a difficult journey but we are here at last. It was thanks to the Brising that we knew anything of this island's existence and...'

'And it is thanks to the Brising that you shall have the chance to speak to the goddess Freyja,' said the women. 'This privilege is given to very few mortals: we hope you are aware of that! We have persuaded the goddess she should hear your request. But be warned – Freyja was furious when she heard that Beorites were coming to see her. However, she has watched your journey with interest and you have impressed her greatly.'

'We've certainly met plenty of dangers!' exclaimed Beorf.

'And you have triumphed over them all. Unwittingly you have thrown fresh light on the conflict between Odin and Freyja. You have accomplished more than you realise. We cannot go into more detail as it relates to the realms of the gods. You may be sure of Freyja's care and consideration from now on!'

Amos and Beorf were completely unaware that Odin had also taken a close interest in their journey. His conflict with Freyja had arisen over the Brisingamen necklace. The great god had accused Freyja of stealing it because four dwarves, Alfrigg, Dvalin, Berling and Grer had each come to him with this accusation. In reality, these four extraordinary jewellers had given the magnificent necklace to Freyja of their own free will to express their admiration of her. They had made it for the goddess so she would be even more beautiful and outshine the sun itself. Loki had disguised himself as each of the dwarves in turn and it was really he who had informed Odin that Freyja had stolen it from them by trickery. He had wanted to create animosity among the gods to suit his own ends. His plan had worked perfectly!

Odin had scolded Freyja severely but she believed him to be jealous of her beauty and thought he wanted the necklace to give to another goddess. Years of warfare had followed with the result that Freyja's curse had fallen on Beorf's race.

As he followed the Beorites' journey Odin soon realised that Loki was trying to disrupt their quest. Intrigued, he had investigated further and discovered the truth. Loki was plotting a revolution in Åsgard and the great god was to be the first to feel its effects. Odin had been taken in by Loki's skill and cunning. Now he understood everything!

'And how can we speak to Freyja?' Amos asked the Brising.

'She will speak to you when she is ready,' the women replied. 'No one gives orders to the gods; it is they who decide the day and the time to visit. Stand in the middle of these ancient tombs and wait.'

'Is that all we have to do then?' asked Beorf, who was quite pleased to be able to rest a while.

'Yes, you just need patience. Good luck.'

Amos and Beorf stepped forward and walked around the huge stone tombs to stand in the middle of the circle. At they did so Amos felt a violent electric shock that knocked him off his feet. A second bolt of lightning followed, then another! The Brising yelled at Beorf:

'Get him out! Carry him away from here! Freyja does not wish to see him. He is not welcome here!'

Beorf took hold of Amos and did as he was told.

'But why does she not want Amos here? He is not dangerous and it is thanks to him that we managed to get here!'

'Because he is a mask-wearer,' declared the women. 'He is not on the side of good or evil but lies between them. The gods will not suffer any mortal who does not follow them. Amos was chosen from thousands of other earth creatures to re-balance the world. Freyja does not like those who try to tell her what to do!'

'You could have warned us,' cried Beorf crossly. 'He might have died!'

'We could have told you, but the goddess ordered us

to remain silent. She wished to punish the mask-wearer!'

Amos opened his eyes and spoke to his friend: 'Wow! Did I dream it or was I just struck by three lightning bolts?'

'You've just avoided being barbecued like a chicken!' Beorf told him. 'I'm afraid it seems that the goddess doesn't like you too much. I'd advise you to stay here quietly and don't move.'

'Good advice, Beorf,' replied Amos with a grin. 'I won't move; you can be sure of that!' Beorf went back to the middle of the stone circle to wait and Amos remained sitting on the grass a little way from it.

All at once the mask-wearer was overcome by a strong premonition that it was absolutely vital that he should take the dragon back to Upsgran. For several minutes this thought completely filled his mind and then it faded away. Where had this idea come from and what had put it into his mind? And why? He hadn't the faintest idea. Some inexplicable power had overwhelmed him. But… it would be just too ridiculous to burden himself with a dragon, surely?

For a start the creature was inaccessible, in a cave right in the heart of a cliff. Second, the beast was nearly dead. If by any chance the dragon had recovered from its wounds, then the creature now guarding the cave would be far more deadly than a griffon. The goddess

Freyja would be delighted if he went back there! And last of all, Sartigan had disagreed entirely with Amos' wisdom in bringing the dragon's egg back from Ramusberget. He could hardly take it back there now it was alive and growing. But the premonition kept coming back: he had to take the dragon back to Upsgran.

Beorf waited patiently for the goddess to speak to him. He stood in the middle of the stone circle until nightfall. When the moon and stars began to appear he decided to lie on the ground. The Beorite was getting irritated; he hated hanging about doing nothing.

'At least if I go to sleep, the time will pass more quickly,' he thought as he stretched out.

Beorf lay on his back gazing at the moon and constellations of stars. He amused himself by joining up the stars with imaginary lines to make pictures. He had managed to draw a chariot and a sword and was beginning to make out a human face. It was a woman's face in profile with a slightly pointed nose. Suddenly, the stars seemed to change position! Beorf rubbed his eyes. Now the profile was full face. It was the face of a very beautiful woman made out of stars and cosmic light. She was wearing a war helmet decorated with short horns. Her hair sparkled with a thousand fires and it drifted out behind her into the darkness. She whispered:

'I am Freyja, young Beorite. You have come all this

way to speak to me, so speak. I am listening. You must excuse me for taking so long to appear before you; I wanted to make myself beautiful for our first meeting.'

Beorf pinched himself. No, he wasn't dreaming! He had to say something…quickly! His throat tightened and his palms were sweaty but he managed to stammer:

'No… no I am… that's all right!'

'What's all right? What do you mean? Humans who come to speak to me are usually better prepared.'

'I am… I am, prepared that is… not human! I am not human, I'm a Beorite. But you already knew that, didn't you? Yes, obviously! I'm here because of the… er… well, what I really do want to ask you is to stop your little game. No! I didn't mean game, I meant stop the curse because… it's not right!'

The goddess gave a soft, tinkling laugh.

'Odin gave you Beorites courage and strength in battle, and faithful hearts, but he certainly didn't bless your race with eloquence or the power of self expression!'

'Oh, no, Beorites can talk all right, but we're not used to talking to gods much. So you see… er… how can I put it? Oh you're right, we're terrible at it, especially when we're nervous!'

'You're very sweet, Beorf Bromanson, and I'm touched that you have come to see me. You have risked your life to come here to plead your people's cause. Your journey has unwittingly changed many things. Odin has given me an apology and he has asked for my hand in marriage. I have accepted.'

'Wow, that's fantastic!' exclaimed Beorf.

'Yes it is fantastic,' smiled the goddess. 'There will be a great ceremony in Åsgard, in the kingdom of the gods. The skies will be lit up with the dancing colours of the aurora borealis and masses of shooting stars.'

'And,' the goddess continued, 'it will also mean that the Beorites whom Odin created will now have a special place in my heart. I have already lifted my curse. Your people are now free to multiply and prosper on Earth.'

'Thank you for your kindness, I am so happy that our journey has served its purpose.'

'You have done well,' agreed Freyja. 'But I cannot let you leave just like that.'

'Why not? asked Beorf in astonishment. 'What have I done to earn your wrath?'

'My wrath? Oh no, I'm not angry with you. I want to do something for you. Sometimes, when a god is especially pleased with one of their followers, they grant them a favour or a miracle, as humans call it.'

'You are going to perform a miracle for me?' exclaimed Beorf, his jaw dropping.

'Yes. I have much to thank you for; it's thanks to you that my quarrel with Odin is over and that he discovered the plot that was being hatched behind his back. It is also thanks to you that I shall soon marry Odin and that I shall now be able to wear the Brisingamen necklace openly and without anger or bitterness.'

'It's… er… also largely thanks to Amos Daragon,' Beorf said meekly.

'You're right, of course, but you must accept that I do not wish to speak of him. Now, if I am counting correctly that means I must owe you four rewards. I will now return these favours, brave little Beorite. I give you Heindall, a magic shield to save you from your enemies. You shall also have Mjollnir, a copy of Thor's magic war hammer. Throw it at anyone who threatens you and it will always return to you.

'Gosh! I must be dreaming!' cried Beorf.

'Wait, I have not yet finished! To show my gratitude to you further, I shall allow you to return home in Skidbladnir, the drakkar of the gods. That will allow you and your friends to get back to Upsgran without more difficulties and to avoid possible problems from Loki. We are keeping an eye on him but one never knows.'

'Thank you so much.'

'Allow me to finish before you thank me. Now for the miracle! Do you remember seeing a falling star recently?'

'Yes, I was on the Kelpies' ship with Amos and he told me to make a wish.'

'What did you wish for?'

'I wished I could see Medusa again!' sighed Beorf wide-eyed. His heart was pounding.

'Well, this is my final favour.' said Freyja. 'You shall see your friend Medusa alive again. Be worthy of the gifts I give you and pray for my happiness with Odin. We shall both be watching you. Wake up now!'

Beorf opened his eyes to find the sun shining on him.

'Oh no!' he yelled. 'I was dreaming!'

He slapped his hand down in disappointment and struck something lying beside him. It was a weapon – a superb war hammer. It was about sixty centimetres long and the upper part was decorated with a twin-headed eagle. The handle was made of oak finely carved with runes. He turned to the other side and saw a shield glittering in the sunlight. It was made of gold and bore the image of a snarling bear. The boy pinched himself again. He wasn't sure whether he was awake or not.

But when he sat up Beorf got an even bigger surprise. At his feet, someone wrapped in a cloak began to stir. Surely he was dreaming, but he wasn't – it really was Medusa!

CHAPTER SEVENTEEN

THE GORGON RETURNS

Beorf yelled at the top of his voice: 'Amos! Come here, Amos!' The young mask-wearer was nearby. He had spent the night asleep on the grass and was wet with dew. He lifted his head in surprise and saw his friend dancing up and down in the middle of the stone circle.

'What's going on Beorf? Why are you so excited?' shouted the boy.

'Because it's a miracle!' cried the manimal. 'It's a miracle! She's here! She has come back! Medusa is here! Right here!'

'He's up to his tricks,' Amos muttered, slowly getting to his feet.

'Come on, Amos! Hurry up!' Beorf yelled.

'If you remember rightly, I'm not exactly welcome in the circle, so if you don't mind, I'll wait here for you.'

'I'm coming! I'm coming!'

Amos could now see that his friend was holding a magnificent shield and had a strange weapon hanging from his belt. And Beorf had just helped someone to stand up. Slowly they walked towards the mask-wearer. This figure appeared to be a young girl with green skin and…

'Medusa!' yelled Amos. 'But that's impossible! Medusa! I must be dreaming!'

'No, you're not dreaming, Amos, it's really her,' Beorf told him as he helped the girl to sit down.

'Amos? Beorf?' she said, bewildered. 'Is it really you? What am I doing here? Did we escape from Karmakas castle? And Great Bratel? A mirror! I remember a mirror.'

'This is unbelievable, Beorf!' cried Amos. 'A shield, a fine new war hammer and Medusa! How on earth…'

'I don't understand what's happening, but I've got the most terrible headache,' said Medusa, rubbing her forehead.

'You'd better explain, Beorf. I'm completely in the dark,' exclaimed Amos.

'Please tell me,' repeated the young Gorgon. 'I was in the castle of a Naga wizard and now I am here, sitting on wet grass in the middle of nowhere with birds singing all round me.'

'Well,' said Beorf, 'I'd better tell you my extraordinary story and make you envious!'

He began by describing the face that had appeared in the stars and went on to tell them about his talk with the goddess Freyja omitting, of course, any mention of his nervous babbling. He told them about the impending marriage between Freyja and Odin, and about the favours she had granted him: the shield, the war hammer, the drakkar and bringing Medusa back to life.

The young Gorgon interrupted: 'You talk of shooting stars and wishes and… bringing me back to life? If I understand you properly, then I must have been dead! Is that right?'

'Dead as the dust!' answered Amos. 'At Great Bratel you died when you looked at your own reflection in Junos's mirror; you had stolen it, remember?'

'Yes, I remember now…' said the young Gorgon. 'Karmakas had forced me to turn Beorf into stone. It was the only way to break the spell. I chose to sacrifice my own life to save him. But where are we now?'

'Far away from Great Bratel!' exclaimed Beorf. 'We're on Freyja's island, right in the middle of nowhere!'

'You're not joking there,' said Amos with a grin.

'I want you to explain something, Beorf,' said Medusa, keeping her eyes hidden under her hood. 'You wanted to see me again even though I had turned you to stone. I betrayed you, Beorf and you… you still thought about me in spite of everything?'

'That's what friendship means, Medusa,' he replied. 'Sometimes you have to forgive.'

'What has happened since I died?' asked the Gorgon. The two boys laughed heartily.

'Oh,' grinned Medusa. 'As much as that?'

'More than you could ever imagine!' smiled the mask-wearer.

'Amos even fell in love with a mermaid. She just called him "handsome" a few times and that was it; he was in love!'

Amos retaliated: 'And you can't go without food for even half a day without turning nasty!'

'That reminds me, I'm hungry now!' laughed Beorf.

'Tell me everything right from the beginning, I'm dying to know!'

The boys told Medusa about all their adventures: the return of Yaune the Purifier, Lolya, the Red Caps, their journey to Ramusberget and the dragon's egg. They told her about the curse on the Beorites of Upsgran, about Sartigan and Amos' masks of power. Stories about the fairies of Tarkasis, Junos, Frilla's capture and the death of Urban all came out. When they had finished, Medusa exclaimed:

'All that has happened in one year! That's incredible!'

Amos suddenly felt ill. He turned on his side and threw up.

'What's wrong?' asked Beorf.

'Are you all right?' asked Medusa.

'No, I'm not. Something is tearing at my heart and soul. I've got a feeling deep inside me, urging me to go back to the cave to help the dragon. I've got to take it back to Upsgran, but I don't know why. The more I shun the idea as impossible, the sicker I feel! It's hard to understand! The creature is dangerous and very aggressive. Sartigan was right: dragons are violent creatures, created to destroy and kill.'

'I've got an idea,' said Medusa. 'We can go back to see this dragon. If it is too dangerous, I can look it in the eye and turn it to stone. What do you think? I can help, now I'm here!'

'It's a great idea!' agreed Amos. 'That way I can clear my conscience and I can see if these intuitions of mine make any sense.'

'Just one small problem,' Beorf cut in. 'How are we going to get there? Don't forget that the cave is half way down a cliff, getting down there without a rope would be suicide.'

'But I can help there, too!' cried Medusa. 'You've forgotten that I have wings under my cloak. I can't fly like a bird, but I can glide. I can easily launch myself off the cliff and glide down using wind thermals. And if the wind drops Amos can always help, can't he?'

'It's lucky you came back to join us Medusa!' cried Amos gratefully.

'I couldn't agree more!' cried Beorf with a huge smile.

'Well, we can't hang about here, let's get going!' cried the Gorgon. 'I've adventures to catch up on!'

The three friends, united once more, walked towards the cliff top. The wind was blowing hard and hundreds of big white birds with yellow heads sailed overhead.

'There's plenty of wind!' Medusa assured them. 'If you want, I can throw myself off and glide down to the cave. Once I'm inside I'll have a look round and I'll signal to you! Is that all right?'

'Perfect!' replied Amos, 'I'll stand by in case the wind drops.'

'And I, well… I'll just keep my fingers crossed!' said Beorf.

The Gorgon turned to face the edge of the cliff and slipped off her cloak. The boys watched her spread her large wings. Her serpent-hair flew up in the wind. In the strong sunlight the serpents wound themselves into sinuous, intertwining loops that shone like gold. For a few seconds this magnificent and terrifying vision transfixed Amos and Beorf.

'I'm going!' cried Medusa.

The Gorgon spread her wings and plunged over the

edge of the cliff. She had no trouble adjusting to the strength of the wind and skilfully anticipated the thermals and their sudden changes of direction. She manoeuvred herself carefully towards the narrow cave entrance and landed in the griffon's lair. Quickly folding her wings she slipped easily through the opening.

'Mission accomplished,' she said to herself. 'Now let's see if the dragon is still here!'

Medusa stepped over the griffon's lifeless body and slowly edged to the back of the cave. Her attention was caught by the sound of laboured breathing. The dragon was still there, hidden among the horse bones. Its body, covered with clotted blood and huge open wounds, was shaken intermittently by sudden spasms. Its breathing was very shallow. With great effort, it half-opened one eye before collapsing back into unconsciousness.

'Hmm, you're in quite a state!' murmured Medusa as she bent over it.

She stroked the dragon's head, then signalled to Amos and Beorf that everything was all right. The boys, who'd been anxious about her, were relieved to see her signal.

'How can I get back up there?' she wondered, scratching her head.

Looking around, she spotted the large wooden chest. She made a quick estimate of the dragon's size and had an idea. The Gorgon tipped all the potions, phials and elixirs out of the chest. She only kept the notebook and the glass jar containing a heart, deciding that a book and a heart were too important to leave behind.

Then the Gorgon took hold of the dragon and dragged it to the chest. The creature was floppy and practically lifeless so offered no resistance. Although barely a month old it was quite heavy and Medusa had trouble curling it round to fit Baba Yaga's chest. The little dragon looked uncomfortable but it was the best she could do. It was unconscious and struggling to breathe as she fastened down the lid.

'Now it's up to you, Amos!' she said to herself. 'I hope your concentration has improved!'

The Gorgon dragged the chest to the cave entrance and took a firm grip on both its handles. Two golden snakes detached themselves from her hair and slid down her arms. They wrapped themselves around her hands like ropes to strengthen her grip and stop her dropping the chest in mid- flight.

Medusa stood upright with great difficulty, spread her wings again and launched herself from the cliff. She was too heavy and immediately started to plunge dangerously downward. Panic-stricken, she tried to stop herself falling by trapping more wind under her wings. It was impossible! She was just too heavy and unbalanced to control her descent.

Amos saw he had to act fast to save her. He closed his

eyes and violently flung his hands skyward. A huge gust of wind swept in off the sea filling the Gorgon's wings and lifting her upward. The mask-wearer created several more gusts of wind and Medusa shot up at lightning speed. Her heart was in her mouth as she hovered over the cliff top.

Amos held her in position but she just could not manoeuvre herself to land. The gusts of wind were unpredictable and the weight of the chest made it difficult for her to control her wings.

Beorf grabbed Medusa's abandoned cloak and tied it to the handle of his war hammer, muttering to himself:

'Freyja said it would always come back to me, now I'll find out if it's true!' The boy threw the hammer towards Medusa and called out:

'Grab hold of the cloak!'

The weapon almost struck her, but the serpents in her hair instantly stretched towards it and hundreds of little mouths caught hold of the fabric. As if by magic, Beorf's hammer swivelled in mid-air and headed back to its master, bringing Medusa with it.

Down Medusa tumbled, landing head first in the grass. She dropped the chest and ended up on her back with her legs in the air, but she was safe!

'Are you ok, Medusa?' asked Amos dashing towards her.

'Stay where you are!' she screamed. 'Don't come near me! I have nothing to hide my eyes. I daren't risk you looking directly at me. Tell Beorf to bring my cloak, quickly!'

'Catch!' said Beorf, throwing it towards her. 'This hammer really works. It's fantastic! Did you see how it came back, Amos?'

'It is fantastic!' exclaimed the mask-wearer. 'That was fast thinking, Beorf. What a great idea! If it hadn't been for you, Medusa would still be spinning in mid-air.'

'We make a good team,' observed Beorf as he helped the Gorgon to her feet.

'Yes,' agreed Medusa, adjusting her cloak. 'I was sure I was going to fall into the sea. Thank you both! Now, let's look at the dragon. He's in the chest but it will be a miracle if he's survived that landing!'

The dragon was still alive. Its body was curled up with its tail tucked underneath it. It was only just breathing and didn't look as if it could survive much longer.

'Right,' said Amos taking stock of the situation. 'We must leave this island as soon as possible and rescue our Beorite friends stuck out at sea. Beorf, you said that Freyja wanted us to return to Upsgran in Skidbladnir, the gods' drakkar? In that case where is the blessed ship?'

With a smile, Beorf took him gently by the chin and turned his head to face inland.

'It's right here!'

CHAPTER EIGHTEEN

SKIDBLADNIR

Skidbladnir was on the grass in front of them, sparkling in the sunshine. Its mighty hull was blood red and decorated with gold and silver designs, precious stones and carvings dedicated to famous warriors. Its dazzling white sail was edged with bands of runic inscriptions. The ship was hung with fine shields depicting famous Nordic victories, skilfully crafted by dwarves. Its wooden figurehead was in the shape of a dragon's head rearing up in readiness to bite. As the three youngsters approached, it came to life:

'Good day, I am Skidbladnir and I shall take you back to the mainland! Climb aboard and make yourselves at home!'

A gangplank was slowly lowered on the starboard side. Beorf muttered as he climbed on deck:

'I hope there's something to eat on this old tub! I'm beginning to feel ravenous!'

'You will find everything a Beorite could possibly desire!' replied the figurehead. 'There's a table on the lower deck that will serve anything you want: fruit, meat, vegetables and cakes! Help yourselves!'

'Oh… er… thanks very much,' mumbled the boy in embarrassment.

'Are there any beetles and maggots?' asked the Gorgon, laughing.

'Certainly,' replied the figurehead. 'I adapt myself to the tastes of all my passengers and you, too, will find all your favourite dishes waiting for you. The Nordic gods pride themselves on satisfying all those who travel on Skidbladnir.'

'We shall enjoy the journey, then!' cried Amos.

'Shall I bring up the chest?' asked the figurehead.

'Yes please,' replied Amos.

Opening its mouth, the figurehead took the chest between its wooden teeth and placed it carefully on the deck.

'While you are aboard Skidbladnir the passage of time changes,' it explained. 'One hour of travelling on the drakkar lasts one second in the world of men. That is why the ship can travel so fast. Are we still bound for Upsgran?'

'Yes,' replied Amos. 'But first can we pick up our friends on the way? They are drifting in a three-masted ship. Can we also search for three warriors lost at sea, three of the Beorite crew?'

'Your friends are no longer there,' replied the figurehead. 'Did no one tell you?'

'What do you mean, not there?' asked Beorf, anxiously. 'Where are they then? We must find them, wherever they are!'

'You don't understand, young Beorite,' the wooden dragon explained. 'I carried them to Åsgard myself, to the kingdom of the gods. Piotr the Giant felled an enormous sea serpent single-handedly. Unfortunately he did not survive his wounds. Helmic and Aldred were both drowned by mermen summoned by Loki to take revenge on those brave warriors. Beorites cannot fight well in water so, in spite of their efforts, they were most savagely murdered. Rutha, Hulot, Banry and the Azulson brothers, Goy and Kasso, also met their deaths at the hands of the mermen at the bottom of the ocean. They, too, fought valiantly but in vain. They all died quickly, without suffering. The Beorites' fate was sealed by Loki's will. I wouldn't like to be there when Odin gets his hands on him, he may be punished...'

Amos and Beorf wept as they heard what had happened to their friends.

'May be punished!' roared the grief-stricken mask-wearer. 'Don't the gods understand anything? Are we just pawns to them, chess pieces to be sacrificed at their whim? Beorf and I have lost the truest of friends. People we loved with all our heart! Loki deliberately caused the deaths of these eight people and he just... may be punished!'

'But eight people is nothing!' replied Skidbladnir. 'Many more than that are killed fighting for their gods; wars between the gods have caused thousands of deaths. Why should the gods punish Loki for eight mortals?'

'Is that all we are to them!' exclaimed Amos, 'just mere mortals of no worth, whose fate depends purely on the gods' good grace? Is that all we are?'

'Yes,' said the figurehead, 'you are insignificant to the gods of this world. You are just foot soldiers that they use to fight their battles. The Earth is one enormous battlefield, filled with strange creatures. Every day you fight, you kill and murder your neighbours in the name of the gods. Didn't you yourself kill goblins? And a dragon? And what about the way Beorf slaughtered Gorgons at Great Bratel?'

'But we were defending ourselves!' retorted Beorf. 'Our violence was in response to aggression. We had no choice!'

'There is always a choice!' the figurehead assured him rather patronisingly.

'Well, if that's true, then I've made my choice! I'm getting off this ship. I don't need gods and their morality or their lectures and favours. I am a mortal and I choose to take care of my own fate without waiting for any god. My mission is to re-balance the Earth and that is why I don't want any favours from Freyja or Odin! I ask nothing of any god, good or evil. From now on, my quest to establish balance in the world will mean struggling against the gods. Striving to give all the Earth's creatures a world in their own image, not one made by the will of any god!'

'Blasphemer!' cried Skidbladnir indignantly. 'You must choose whose side you are on, you cannot stay neutral and live without any allegiance. You can't choose. You're only a mortal! Stay, or else.'

'Or else what?' yelled Amos. 'Try and keep me here and see how a mere mortal can have you in flames with a click of his fingers. Don't ever threaten me or you'll suffer the consequences. If the lives of eight Beorites, eight of my friends, don't count, well Skidbladnir's existence must matter little to the gods either. You must be just as disposable as any human, gnome or fairy! I'm going, don't even think of trying to stop me!'

Amos left the ship and walked angrily towards the cliff top. The figurehead looked away and did nothing to stop him. As he walked, Amos could still hear Banry's songs and he pictured Hulot's gentle face. He remembered Helmic's energy, Goy's and Kasso's quarrels, and Rutha's tenderness. He thought of the courage of Piotr and Aldred, and imagined them all at some eternal banquet, united in death.

The mask-wearer had tears in his eyes and his heart was heavy. He had lost true friends, people who had welcomed him as one of their own and who truly loved him.

'I'm getting off, too!' said the Gorgon decisively. 'Freyja brought me back to life and I am very grateful, but in spite of that I have no wish to bow to the will of the gods. The gods of the Gorgons never showed me the meaning of friendship. It was Amos and Beorf who made me a better creature, no one else. I owe the gods nothing. I owe everything to those who try to understand and respect me, even if I am different! Don't stop me either or I might just look you in the eye. A blink from me would turn you to stone.'

The young Gorgon climbed down from the ship with her head held high.

Skidbladnir turned to Beorf and said smugly: 'Well then, young Beorite, I shall take you home. Let's go, son of Odin!'

'I am no son of Odin,' replied Beorf angrily. 'I am the son of Evan and Hanna Bromanson.'

He dropped the hammer and shield that Freyja had given him: 'You can give these back to the goddess. I don't want them! I understand a lot of things now. Our people are a proud race! It's because of a stupid quarrel over a necklace that my people's future was jeopardised by a curse. A trivial misunderstanding among the gods led to the death of my parents, my friends and hundreds of Beorite infants. And all for what? For a necklace!

'Tell Freyja that the Bromanson family cannot be bought with magic toys. I came to plead my people's cause, but I will never forget that Odin and Freyja have made me lose people I loved with all my heart. I will never fight for the gods or for the cause of good or evil. I shall fight side by side with my friends to free the world from the gods' power. I would rather starve than travel on my enemies' ship.'

Beorf left the hammer and shield behind; he no longer needed them. A true Beorite fights with his claws, his teeth and his courage – which he already had. Beorf picked up the chest with the dragon inside and climbed down to join his friends.

Behind them Skidbladnir slipped slowly away.

The three friends, standing side by, stared blankly out to the ocean. The water stretched as far as they could see. Silently they each reflected upon their situation until Beorf remarked:

'Well, we really are in trouble, now!'

Amos and Medusa burst out laughing.

'I'd say we're right up to our necks in it,' groaned Amos.

'Perhaps even deeper,' added Medusa.

'And I'm starving…,' said the manimal, solemnly.

'That's typical!' cried the mask-wearer, laughing. 'Here we are, in the middle of nowhere, thousands of miles from home, we've just turned all the gods in the world against us, lost our dearest friends and thrown away our only chance of getting back to Upsgran... and you're hungry!'

'That's another reason I feel peckish,' retorted the Beorite. 'Turning the gods against you gives you an appetite!'

'I know a good recipe for earthworm soup!' cried the Gorgon.

'Do you know what?' answered Beorf. 'I really don't feel hungry any more!'

'Well, then. Allow me to invite you to supper!' cried a high-pitched little voice from behind them.

Medusa, Beorf and Amos turned. Standing in the long grass was a little man, less than a metre in height, with a red beard and hair. He was smoking a long, curved white pipe. Half his teeth were rotten, hairs stuck out of his ears and he had a firm round belly. He wore a long green coat full of holes and patches, a wide leather belt and a leather hat that made him look like a mushroom.

'Good morrning! My name is Flag Marrtan Mac Heklagrrroen and the inhabitants of this island owe you our grrrratitude! You can call me Flag!'

'Pleased to meet you, Flag! My name is Amos and this is Beorf and Medusa,' said the mask-wearer cheerfully. 'What reason do you have to be grateful to us?'

'Come and eat first!' said Flag. 'You can't talk on an

empty stomach. You must get yourr strrrength back. You can trrust me, you arre in good hands. We Leprechauns are peaceful, frriendly folk.'

'Lead on,' cried Beorf, patting his belly. 'My stomach is grumbling!'

Carrying the chest between them, the three friends followed this strange little man. Amos was sorry he could no longer shrink the bulky chest and the dragon. Wild horses galloped around them without coming too close. Amos, Beorf and Medusa had been struggling through the long grass for about twenty minutes when Flag stopped and lifted up a trapdoor in the ground.

'Herre we arre! Please step this way!' said the Leprechaun.

The trapdoor was well hidden in the grass at the far western end of the island. Amos wondered how the little ginger man had managed to find it so easily. There were no landmarks, signs or any other clues; it was so well camouflaged that it was undetectable.

'Leave the chest herre,' Flag suggested. 'My frriends will come and brring it down to you! We know what is in it and we will take grreat carre of it!'

'Have you been watching us?' asked Amos, curiously.

'In a mannerr of speaking, yes! From the time you arrived in the grriffon's talons until you rrefused to travel in Skidbladnirrr. Come in and mind your heads!'

A long dark passageway led underground. The

youngsters went along it and climbed cautiously down a steep ladder. The Leprechaun closed the trapdoor behind him.

After a seemingly endless descent in complete darkness Amos, who was leading, came out into a brightly lit cavern. He put his hands to his eyes to shield them from the sudden brightness. A loud clapping noise filled the room! The applause of hundreds of over-excited Leprechauns rang out to greet the three friends.

CHAPTER NINETEEN

THE LEPRECHAUNS' MACHINE

There were Leprechauns everywhere! Hundreds of little red-haired men with beards and pipes, together with their wives and children, were shouting their heads off. The cave was set out like a giant theatre. There was an orchestra pit, theatre boxes carved into the rocks, stalls and a huge balcony. All the seats were full, there wasn't a space to be found anywhere!

An ingenious system of mirrors directed sunlight into the cave, dazzling Beorf and Medusa with its blinding light. Flag stepped in front of the young people and walked onto the stage.

'My fellow Leprrrechauns!' he began forcefully.

Slowly, their joyful cries died down.

'My fellow Leprrrechauns!' Flag repeated in a much louder voice. 'I know it is harrd for a Leprrechaun to be quiet but...'

'Hush!' cried several voices from the audience. 'Hush!'

'Thank you!' continued Flag, relighting his pipe. 'May I prresent our saviourrs!'

Once again the crowd began to roar! Cries, whistles and applause rang out from all sides! Flag tried to calm the delirious Leprechauns:

'Be quiet! That's enough! Let me speak!'

It was impossible to control them. For several minutes Flag tried to speak, but in vain! The little man was red with anger and began to insult the crowd. He waved his arms and jumped up and down till he was breathless.

This spectacle only served to make the crowd worse. The sight of their chief, Flag Martan Mac Heklagroen leaping up and down like a demented puppet made them laugh until tears ran down their cheeks. Several began playing musical instruments and singing along. Finally, beside himself with rage, Flag turned his back to the audience, dropped his trousers and stuck his bottom out. This provoked a new wave of hysterical shouts and howls fit to make the island shake. Flag pulled up his trousers and hurled his clogs into the crowd before calling to his companions:

'They arre impossible! Follow me!'

The friends stood up and followed Flag down another corridor lit by little lamps fixed to the wall. Amos realised that the island must be riddled with passages, galleries and corridors. Dozens of ladders led up and down on all sides. Flag guided them confidently through the maze of twisting paths until they came into a large room. Comfy cushions were scattered around a table groaning with food. Without waiting to be asked, Beorf began tucking in.

'Tuck in, all of you!' cried Flag, still flustered by his people's behaviour. 'I shall join you!'

'Thank you,' replied Amos. 'We'd like nothing better!'

'Mmm yes,' said Beorf, his mouth stuffed with nut cake.

'Can you explain to us what is going on here,' asked the young mask-wearer politely. 'I'd like to know how we can possibly be your saviours. I really don't think we have done anything for you.'

Flag began to tell them in detail about the history of the island's Leprechauns. The story started in the mists of time, when Freyja's island belonged to the Leprechauns.

'Our people lived above ground in sweet little thatched cottages. They used to breed horses and galloped about on them all day long. They were perfectly happy on their small plot of land in the middle of the ocean. One day, however, Freyja decided to make the island her refuge, her earthly temple. She sent the

Valkyrie, fierce warrior maidens riding winged horses, to rid the island of the "ginger vermin" who inhabited it. Thousands of Leprechauns were killed and thrown off the cliffs. Legend has it that the souls of the dead came back as birds to curse the goddess Freyja with their constant cries.

'The survivors took refuge in the caves but Freyja brought a griffon to the island to guard it. It was this griffon that forced the Leprechauns to stop living above ground and they began hollowing out tunnels to live in. For generations the Leprechauns only dared to creep out occasionally to watch their horses running wild among the long grass. Freyja had condemned them to live their lives hidden away in the darkness. The powerful goddess had scorned their gods and taken over their island. The Leprechauns always referred to her as "the mortal", refusing to speak her name.

'Left to their own devices the Leprechauns became very resourceful and inventive. They built machines to dig out the earth, they booby-trapped doors to trick the griffon, they created their own lighting systems based on earth oil, ovens that used magnifying glasses, cookers powered by the sun and underground greenhouses to grow huge quantities of vegetables. In spite of their fun-loving disposition, the little people managed to work miracles. They regained control of their own destiny and quickly adapted to their new environment.

'For years we've wanted to force Freyja to leave the island, first by killing off her griffon. To our great joy, you did it for us! That is why we see you as heroes! Now, by refusing Freyja's favours, you're twice as heroic in our eyes. My Leprechaun spies have seen everything and reported it back to me.'

But Medusa seemed to unsettle Flag. He avoided looking at her and didn't answer her questions. Her hooded eyes seemed to make him uneasy. Amos realised this was a problem and explained to the Leprechaun chief that Medusa's eyes were the very last thing any one should want to look at. The Gorgon explained that she had the power to turn all living creatures into stone. She told him how hard it was to keep her head hooded and lowered at all times for fear of meeting someone's gaze.

'If I underrstand you, as long as one does not see your eyes, therre is no dangerr?'

'That's right!' agreed Medusa, smiling.

'Just give me a few minutes,' said the little man. 'I think I can solve yourr prroblem!'

Flag left the room and quickly came back with three Leprechauns. They asked Medusa to close her eyes and remove her hood. The Gorgon felt great confidence in Flag and did as she was asked. The three little men took a series of measurements of her head, discussed them quietly, then left the room talking about a certain 'sand stone' that was actually transparent.

'What's happening?' asked Medusa as she put on her hood again.

'The Leprrechauns are going to make you a prresent!' answered Flag. 'Just rrelax for a while, we'll soon be rready to go!'

'Where?' asked Amos.

'We'rre going to take you home!' replied the little man.

'How?' asked Amos.

'Laterr,' answered Flag, 'you'll see laterr! Rrest now and I'll come and get you when we arre rready. Therre's water over there and blankets just herre if you want to wash. If you want fresh air there's a camouflaged window that opens onto the cliff. Overr there, do you see? But… what's that noise?'

'That's Beorf snoring,' explained Amos. 'As soon as his stomach's full his eyes close automatically!'

'Phew! That's a relief,' murmured the Leprechaun as he left the room. 'I thought it was an earthquake.'

Amos was still eating but Medusa hardly ate a thing. She didn't care for the food of other races, preferring dishes made from insects. Fortunately she'd found some as they'd walked through the underground passages and she was no longer hungry.

The mask-wearer went off to wash and quickly saw that Medusa had also fallen asleep. Amos opened the window and looked out to sea. The sun was slipping down below the horizon. The air was fresh and the ocean smelled wonderful! Untying his hair, he shook it free. As he gazed into the distance he thought of his mother. He remembered her laughing and playing with him at their cottage in the kingdom of Omain. He thought of Urban, too, and how his father had been so cruelly murdered by the Red Caps. Amos often had flashbacks of that horrible scene. A great emptiness filled his heart. Amos had survived some extraordinary adventures, but he still missed his family dreadfully. He began to weep.

In spite of his friends' company, he suddenly felt terribly alone and vulnerable. He was only thirteen years old and his mission seemed to be getting harder and harder to bear. Would it always be like this – one adventure after another without stopping? Would everyone he loved die or disappear?

'I think I'd like to turn back the clock and return to Omain,' he said to himself. 'I'm beginning to regret ever having met Crivannia in the Bay of Caves. I wish it were all just a dream so that everything could stop and become ordinary again. No wild creatures, no bullying gods and no more dangers to face.'

Amos was suddenly exhausted. He flopped heavily on to the cushions and was asleep as soon as his eyes closed. Lolya's face appeared to him. His friend looked splendid as she spoke calmly to him:

'Amos, I am so glad to be able to speak to you at last. I know your mother's whereabouts and she needs help. Come back soon. We must help her. I know you will think this is just a dream but it really is me talking to you. I am in Upsgran awaiting your return. I've tried to contact you for days but you never sleep deeply enough. Bring the dragon back with you. It was me who made you want to save the creature. I have come back to help you and Beorf. He will tell you that you have not imagined this message! This is not a dream. Good night, Amos. I can't wait to see you both again.'

The young mask-wearer opened his eyes suddenly. A pale morning light filled the room. Beorf woke a few seconds after Amos. He rubbed his eyes and said sleepily:

'I've had such a strange dream! Lolya was asking me to give you a message. She kept saying: "This is not a dream. This is not a dream." Does that mean anything to you?'

'Yes,' said Amos. 'I had my doubts but it's clear now!'

'Where's Medusa?' asked Beorf.

'I don't know…' replied the mask-wearer, plaiting his hair again. 'She was here last night when I fell asleep. She can't be far!'

'She's probably gone to find herself a few juicy beetles to eat. She's a wonderful girl but I hate her choice of food!'

'If we're lucky, she might bring us back a few insects!'

At that moment Flag Martan Mac Heklagroen came in leading Medusa by the hand. Behind them came three other Leprechauns, heads held high and looking very pleased with themselves. The young Gorgon's face was heavily hooded as usual, but she seemed to be having problems seeing where she was going.

'We should like to have your opinion, gentlemen!' declared the little ginger man.

'What about?'

'About this!' cried Flag, pulling back the Gorgon's hood.

Instinctively, Beorf and Amos covered their eyes.

'There's no need for that,' Medusa reassured them, 'I... I'm... well, you can look!'

The Gorgon had something very strange fastened over the top of her head to which spectacles were attached. These had red lenses that reflected light back so that her eyes could not be seen. The spectacles were beautifully made and suited her face and the greenish colour of her skin.

'How wonderful!' exclaimed Amos.

'You look lovely!' added Beorf.

'And it's practical,' she said, 'I can see through the glass! I don't need to hide my eyes any more. I can look at you now without any risk of…'

'Turning us into pigeon perches!' laughed Amos.

'Exactly!' smiled Medusa, shyly.

'She's not quite used to them yet,' explained Flag, 'but in a few days time herr sight will adjust.'

'And you'll be able to chase beetles as well as ever!' joked Beorf.

'Yes, and I'll make you two eat them!' she laughed.

'Enough of this nonsense, follow me,' ordered Flag cheerfully. 'We've got anotherr surrrprrrise for you! Come on, on your feet!'

The boys sprang to their feet and they all trooped down more long passageways and up and down steep staircases. As he walked Beorf could hear the sound of someone chewing. He glanced over his shoulder to see Medusa right behind him with her mouth full.

'I was a bit peckish,' she said. 'Do you want one? They're nice and juicy!'

'Ugh!' shuddered Beorf. 'Do you remember when we met at Great Bratel? It was in the cave and you were eating spiders. I never said anything but it made me feel sick!'

'I like grasshoppers too, and earthworms and nice fat bumblebees!' answered Medusa, who took a wicked delight in teasing him. 'But what I really like…'

'No! Stop!' he begged. 'I don't want to hear anymore!'

'What a pity,' said the young Gorgon mockingly.

They emerged into a huge cavern hewn out of the rock. They could see the sky through a large hole cut into the ceiling. Hundreds of Leprechauns were working on a strange machine.

Flag explained that it was a flying machine. He had invented it himself and was very proud of it, especially its name: The Flagmobile!

His flying machine consisted of a balloon full of hot air. By experimenting, Flag had discovered an indisputable law of physics: that is, hot air rises and cold air falls. He couldn't quite explain it, but he was certain that if he could keep the balloon filled with hot air, it would fly. He had created The Flagmobile in order to attack the griffon. But now the creature was dead he proposed flying Medusa and the boys back to the mainland.

Suspended from the balloon was an old Viking boat in which the chest containing the young dragon had already been placed. An oil-burning blacksmith's forge pumped hot air up into the billowing shape above it. At the rear was a big propeller worked by pedals. There was enough food on board for the great journey and the machine was ready to depart.

The Leprechauns applauded as the party climbed on

board. Flag ordered them to cut the cables holding The Flagmobile but the craft didn't budge! There was a murmur of disappointment from the crowd.

'I don't understand,' he cried, shaking his head. 'We should be flying!'

'Perhaps we are too heavy for it,' suggested Amos.

'It would be too dangerrous for the burrner to be any hotter.' said Flag. 'I've calculated the amount of oil we need and if we use more I shan't everr be able to come back!'

'Maybe I can help,' said Amos. 'We can save oil and take off very fast!'

The young mask-wearer concentrated hard, raised one hand towards the balloon and placed his other hand just above the burner. Using his powers over fire and air, Amos absorbed heat in one hand and expelled it with the other to make a steady stream of hot air.

A hot whirlwind inflated the balloon.

Amos kept his magic steady for several minutes until, at last, they gradually began to move. The Leprechauns hooted with joy! Flag's invention had worked! The balloon doubled in size and looked ready to burst. Then it slowly lifted off, just grazing the edge of the opening in the cave roof.

'Therre you arre!' cried its delighted inventor. 'I knew it would worrk! I just knew it!'

'With a little help from Amos things usually work!' said Medusa under her breath.

The Flagmobile rapidly gained height and soon Freyja's island was just a dot in the ocean. Amos broke off his spell and glanced down.

'We're really high!' he called.

'And I don't much like it!' cried Beorf, clinging to the basket.

'I love it!' shouted the Gorgon. Flag was at the back of the machine pedalling hard to make the big propeller turn. He had made some simple navigational instruments and was trying to find the right direction.

'I'm finding it harrd to get the balloon to face the rright way! The wind is against us!'

'I'll take care of that,' said the mask-wearer, raising his right hand.

Immediately a gust of wind turned The Flagmobile the way it should go.

'It's easy!' called Amos. 'Let's save oil for your journey home, Flag. I'll take care of heating the air for the balloon whenever we lose altitude. If you think we're going off course, just let me know!'

'You'll have to tell me how you do that!' said the Leprechaun. 'You arre a verry surrprrrising boy, young Amos!'

'I'll tell you everything when we have time,' he grinned back.

Just then Medusa spotted a rope that was lying around. She tied one end firmly to the basket and wrapped the other around her waist. Spreading her wings she leapt into the air with a great whoop of delight. While tethered to The Flagmobile she could float along shouting for joy.

'I've always wanted to fly! Yoweee! Its fantastic! I'm flying!'

'She eats insects and she likes flying like a bird,' sighed Beorf, whose stomach was churning. 'She really is a strange girl!'

'Bravo!' yelled Amos, clapping his hands. 'You look wonderful! If you need more wind, just tell me!'

It made the strangest spectacle: a green-skinned girl flying behind a boat, suspended from a gigantic balloon with a little ginger man at the back pedalling for all he was worth! One boy on board was taming the wind and another was half dead with fright. Any birds crossing their path saw the strangest sight of their lives!

CHAPTER TWENTY

THE NEW TEAM

The remainder of the journey passed without problems and The Flagmobile reached the mainland in just a few days. The mask-wearer loved travelling through the clouds. As they flew over the Great Fog Barrier the Grey Man watched them warily. The boy thought of Kasso: from this height the Beorite could have drawn wonderfully accurate maps for his people to use. Not only could Amos see where the islands lay and how the currents ran, but he could also make out great shoals of fish and the whales' migration routes.

Beorf, on the other hand, was in torment. He felt so ill for the whole journey that he couldn't eat a thing and so lost lots of weight. Imprisoned in the flying ship, he swore that his feet would never leave the ground again. He felt sick, couldn't sleep and was almost at the end of his tether despite Medusa's attempts to comfort him.

The little dragon died just before they reached Upsgran, even though Flag had nursed him so carefully. Amos was devastated! He had brought the egg back from the dragon's lair at Ramusberget. The creature was a problem but it was part of his life. He had wanted something better for this wonderful, dangerous beast. He had wanted to save it and mould it into a better, less destructive creature. Sartigan thought it an impossible task, but Amos believed that he could have done it. He was certain that there must be even the tiniest bit of good in the heart of such a creature. The opposite was certainly true of Freyja. The goddess was supposed to be on the side of good! Yet what she had done to the Leprechauns and the Beorites left him in no doubt about her character.

'Are you going to be able to get back safely?' Amos asked Flag as he clambered out of the basket.

'Yes, my dearr frriend!' the little man assured him. 'Don't worry about me. Your magic has saved plenty of oil for me. I have full confidence in The Flagmobile. Take carre of your friend, Beorrf, and I'm verry sorrry about the drrrragon. Take the chest with you; it will be his coffin!'

'Thank you so much for a wonderful journey,' said Medusa kissing Flag on the forehead. 'And thank you for this invention to hide my eyes. What do you call it exactly?'

'Hmmm,' said Flag. 'Well, as Leprrechauns made them and you look so sweet in them, we shall call them "Leprracles". You'rre wearring leprracles my dearr Medusa!'

'That's a great name,' said Amos distractedly, as he watched Beorf rolling in the grass, kissing the ground.

'Goodbye!' cried the Leprechaun chief as he fired his burner for take off. 'I hope your adventurres will bring you back to our island someday!'

'Safe journey!' called Amos and Medusa as The Flagmobile gained height.

'Goodbye!' muttered Beorf, determined never, ever, to have another journey like that.

'Let's go,' said Amos. 'Upsgran isn't far and we've got to tell the villagers that the crew are dead. Let's take the chest with us to give the dragon a proper burial.'

'I won't come with you,' said Medusa. 'With my hair and the colour of my skin and my wings, most other races think I look more like the devil than anything else. I'll stay here at the edge of the woods with the dragon; I'll guard his remains and wait for you to come back. Then we'll see if it's wise to introduce me to your friends.'

'That's a good idea, Medusa. That would probably be best.'

Medusa was sitting quietly on the chest in the middle of the forest when she heard a noise behind her. She turned to find a girl with a spear raised threateningly. The Gorgon nearly jumped out of her skin when she saw her attacker. She had never seen anyone with skin the colour of ebony!

'What are you doing here?' asked Lolya aiming her spear at Medusa. 'Who are you? Why have you got snakes on your head?'

'And who are you?' retorted Medusa, getting ready to tear off her lepracles. 'Why are you threatening me? And why are you wearing so much jewellery?'

'Answer me or take the consequences!' ordered Lolya.

'Make one move and I swear you will regret it!' countered Medusa.

A long silence followed as the girls weighed each other up. Lolya tried to defuse the situation.

'I mean you no harm. I was on my way to Upsgran to welcome my friends. I sensed they had arrived. I live over there.'

The Gorgon replied: 'I am waiting for my friends to come back from the village for me. They're called Beorf and Amos…'

'But… but …' stammered Lolya, dropping her spear. 'That's who I'm on my way to see! Wait a minute. You must be Medusa! Beorf often talked about you when we were in Berrion. He told me you were dead!'

'I was dead!' said Medusa. 'It's a long story. You must be Lolya, then! Amos told me about you when we were on Freyja's island. I'm pleased to meet you. I thought you had gone back to your own country. You're a queen or a princess aren't you?'

'Yes,' the Morgorian replied. 'I went back to Berrion to find Amos, but Junos told me he was here. But it's a long story. It's a pleasure to meet you!'

The two girls shook hands, laughing nervously.

'I'm looking after this chest. It has a dragon in it that…'

'You've got the dragon!' cried Lolya. 'In that chest?'

'Yes, but it's dead. It died on the way back…'

'Show me!' cried Lolya, as she ran to the chest. 'When did it die?'

'Only a few hours ago.'

'Right! Then there's still time! Help me to carry it into the cabin over there, I think I can save it.'

'That's the whole story,' said Amos. 'The curse afflicting the Beorites has been lifted, but Upsgran has paid a high price for Odin and Freyja's dispute.'

A painful silence filled the little inn. The villagers had listened to Amos' account of the journey without flinching. Their chief, Banry Bromanson, had died at sea with his brave crew. Beorite warriors understood the risks of such an adventure. The important thing was that the curse had been lifted and now the Beorite race would have a future once more. Their brave sailors and fearless fighters had not died in vain.

The villagers of Upsgran went on asking questions for several hours.

Beorf and Amos answered as best they could, adding more details or filling in bits of the story they had missed out earlier. When everyone was satisfied Geser Mitson, known as the Stone Marten, stood up and spoke:

'I have fought at the side of Banry, Hulot, Rutha, Piotr, Aldred, Goy and Kasso. I was at the battle of Ramusberget. We shall honour their memory and sing of their exploits for centuries to come. If Banry had needed me I would have gone without hesitation and I would have been honoured to die by his side. Today I have lost my dearest friends and I mourn them.'

Geser had tears in his eyes. He paused for a few moments and then, clearing his throat, he continued: 'But life must go on. We shall need a new chief. Since its beginnings, this village's destiny has always been decided by the Bromansons, a pure-bred Beorite family. No Bromanson leader has ever been ousted, they are faithful of heart and as reliable as the mountains. They have the strength and instinct, the loyalty and character of all great leaders.

'Ill-luck took Evan from us and the sea has now taken Banry. Fortunately fate has brought the last of the line of this glorious family back to us. I propose that a Bromanson takes over the leadership of this village for our own good and for that of generations to come. I propose that Beorf Bromanson shall be our new leader!'

Beorf, who was drinking a glass of goat's milk, almost choked when he heard these last few words.

'I… I can't…,' stammered the boy, trying to catch his breath, 'I'm far too young and I don't know anything about politics.'

'You will do the same as your father and your uncle did,' called out the fat innkeeper, 'you will learn!'

'But I hardly know the village or its people!' cried Beorf, 'in any case I….'

'We need a leader we can trust,' Geser interrupted him. 'You are a Bromanson and your family has always governed us well. In spite of your age, your ancestors' history speaks for you. A tree is judged worthy by its roots and its fruit. You are the best thing that could happen to this village!'

'I propose a vote,' said the fat innkeeper's wife. 'Those in favour of electing Beorf as leader of our village, raise their hand!'

The whole village did as she said. With a single movement they all raised a hand.

'That's unanimous!' exclaimed Geser. 'If you refuse,

Beorf, we shall have to have an election and that will divide us. A united village is a happy village.'

Beorf, completely overwhelmed, turned to Amos murmuring: 'What should I do?'

'You must follow your heart, Beorf,' replied Amos, 'that's what Sartigan would probably tell you. As a matter of fact... where is he? Have you seen him?'

'No I haven't!' replied the young Beorite turning to face the villagers. 'I would ask you, that is... I'd like to put off giving you my decision until after the funeral rites for Banry and the rest of the crew. I think that their memory should be honoured first before a new leader is chosen!'

'That is a wise decision,' agreed Geser. 'You must see that you already bear the marks of a great leader! Your sense of respect and wisdom tell me that Upsgran will do well to have you as leader.'

'Let us prepare for the ceremony,' said a voice from the audience. 'We'll follow our traditions and the rites shall take place in two days time.'

The villagers stood up and left the inn. Beorf, stunned by the Beorites's proposal, did not get up immediately. His legs were like jelly. Amos brought him back to earth by saying:

'Come on, great chief! Let's go and find Sartigan and tell him the good news! We'll collect Medusa on the way.'

Lolya opened the chest. She examined the dragon quickly then asked Medusa to help her lift it out. The young Morgorian fetched seven candles and placed them in a circle around the creature. Then she uttered some incomprehensible words.

'What are you doing, Lolya?' asked the young Gorgon. 'The creature's dead.'

'Ah!' cried the young witch. 'I see Amos didn't tell you everything about me! I've just stopped the dragon's soul from leaving its body to give me more time.'

'Time to do what?' asked Medusa, doubtfully.

'I've already told you,' answered Lolya with a smile. 'I want to bring it back to life!'

Instinctively the Gorgon moved away. So Lolya was a real witch, like Karmakas. Medusa was wary of this kind of magician. They could capture a Gorgon's soul with the greatest of ease and manipulate it like a puppet.

Lolya looked at Medusa. 'Hmmm, I can sense you don't trust me. Your fear is easy to read. Well, don't be frightened. Pass me the notebook from the chest and the jar with the heart, if you would be so kind.'

'I don't mind at all and I'm not afraid of you,' said Medusa nonchalantly.

'That's just as well because I need an assistant!' replied Lolya as she opened Baba Yaga's notebook.

The young Morgorian quickly read through the whole book. She thought quietly for a few moments then said:

'She was certainly a talented witch! This book is an absolute gold mine of recipes for making potions, elixirs and magic ointments. Baba Yaga used great imagination in choosing her ingredients, but her spells are too full of hate, darkness and despair.'

'Do you understand those sorts of things?' asked the astonished Gorgon warily.

'Yes. There are many kinds of magic and witchcraft, but they are all based on the same principles. Even though Baba Yaga was so venomous and enthralled by misery and poisons, I can still grasp the sense of her spells and understand her concoctions.'

'And what kind of magic do you work in?'

'I work with spirits to foretell the future. I combine my own inner forces with the energy from the spirits who are all around us. I can sense things such as, for example, that you don't trust me!'

'Oh…'

'Don't worry. Trust doesn't come easily – it has to be earned. I shall work to gain your trust! Now let's make a start! I think I know who this heart belonged to and I also think I understand how it was bewitched. Pass me that big knife, please.'

The Gorgon did as she was asked and watched as Lolya opened up the dragon's belly. The witch chanted some incomprehensible words. A supernatural creature suddenly appeared beside her in a halo of light. The apparition was like a translucent mist that passed behind Lolya and took hold of her hands to guide them. Together, they gently removed the dragon's heart and replaced it with the one from Baba Yaga's jar. The spirit seemed to be whispering in the young witch's ear while she worked in a semi-trance.

'This Lolya is certainly very powerful!' thought Medusa as she watched. 'I'd rather have her for a friend than an enemy. But I wouldn't mind learning some of her tricks!'

After many hours of careful work, the heart began to beat in the dragon's chest. Black, sulphurous blood began to circulate through its veins once more. The spirit left Lolya and she began to sew up the creature's belly.

'Some of the membranes in the human heart have had to be modified to adapt to this new kind of blood. Now I have to negotiate.'

'Negotiate?'

'Yes. I've got to negotiate for the dragon's life. I have to bargain with a filthy zombie who gets his life force when a soul breaks away from the body.'

'But what was that other "thing" that was around you during the operation?' asked the fascinated Gorgon.

'An astral guide… an ethereal creature. Oh, how can

I describe it to you? There are many "guardians of knowledge" in another dimension that we call "the astral plane". I asked for help with my task and a "guardian" came to help me. It is thanks to him that I was able to give the dragon a new heart.'

'But why did you do that? Why did you want to save it? They are vicious, evil creatures that only bring trouble.'

'Just like Gorgons who know nothing of compassion and friendship,' replied Lolya with a smile, 'sometimes things happen to change a person's heart.'

'I can see that Beorf must have told you our story!' laughed Medusa. 'I understand now what you do and why you do it! I was a good example!'

'I don't know why exactly, but I just knew that I had to save the dragon,' the young Morgorian sounded puzzled. 'I think it will play an important part when Amos comes to re-balance the world. Right, now for that zombie!'

By the time Beorf and Amos reached Sartigan's cabin it was all over. The dragon with its new heart was wrapped up warmly in several blankets and breathing feebly.

Lolya ran to embrace her friends once more. She

Lolya ran to embrace her friends once more. She explained to Amos what had brought her back to him. She told him of her dreams of Frilla, the huge tower and an old man called Sartigan. She told him how she had met Medusa in the forest and transplanted a new heart into the dragon. Amos listened carefully.

'I am so happy to see you again Lolya, and I'm thrilled that you want to join us! I've still got much to do and you will be an enormous help. We shall rest for a bit and then we'll go and look for the tower that haunts your dreams.'

'And we'll rescue your mother and Sartigan,' put in Beorf eagerly.

'Yes, boss!' exclaimed Amos, laughing. 'When a Beorite chief gives an order it must be obeyed!'

'I haven't accepted yet, handsome!' retorted Beorf mockingly. 'Shall I tell Lolya how easily you fall in love with mermaids?'

'Amos? In love?' cried the young girl in surprise.

'Did you say "chief"?' asked Medusa.

'Later...' said Beorf, patting his belly. 'Let's have something to eat. I'm still hungry! I need my stomach to be full if I'm going to think about my future!'

'You're unbelievable Beorf! You're always hungry...'

The mask-wearer's mission had begun in the far-off lands of the Kingdom of Omain. A year after his first visit to the Forest of Tarkasis he already had three masks, three stones of power and a mass of adventures behind him. Now he had three friends by his side ready to help him, three faithful partners who had absolute belief in the importance of his mission.

That evening, as the four companions lay on the damp grass watching the stars, Amos thought there was nothing stronger in the whole world than a friendship that is built on respect. A manimal, a Gorgon, a witch and a mask-wearer would seem to have little in common. But there they all were, laughing together in the moonlight, all believing that they could make a difference to the world. That was faith indeed – the kind of faith that can move mountains!

Glossary of Mythology

THE GODS

Freyja: This Germanic goddess is also known as Freya or Frea. The daughter of Njord the Scandinavian sea god, she symbolises sexual desire and fertility.

Loki: Also known as Lopt, he is the Germanic god of fire. A mischief-maker, he promotes discord and can change his form at will.

Odin: He is the chief god in both Germanic and Scandinavian mythology. He is often seen sitting on his throne from where he keeps watch over the nine worlds. He has two tireless crows as messengers who fly around him at all times. Odin sacrificed an eye so that he could drink from the fountain of wisdom. He presides over the councils of the Nordic gods in his great palace of Valhalla in the fortress of Åsgard.

MYTHICAL PLACES & MAGICAL OBJECTS

Åsgard: The fabulous city of the Åsir – the gods headed by Odin. The Vanir, such as Freyja, inhabited Vanaheim. Åsgard's huge walls were built by Hrimthurs, who asked for Freyja's hand as reward for his eighteen months' work but was never granted his wish.

Mjöllnir: The name of the god Thor's war hammer. The hammer symbolised destruction, fertility and rebirth. The god used it to protect Åsgard from the ice giants, enemies of the gods.

Skidbladnir: A marvellous drakkar (longship) built by skilful dwarves as the gods' warship. Cloudlike, it could travel on land, sea and in the air.

Valhalla: The Viking heaven where true heroes, that is those who died in valiant combat, feasted night and day.

Yggdrasil: The cosmic ash tree was at the centre of the universe in Germanic and Scandinavian mythology. The tree supported the nine worlds that included the three human kingdoms, the lands of the light-haired elves and dwarves, the lands of the dark-haired elves and the frozen lands of the giants.

LEGENDARY CREATURES

The Brising: Also known as Bristling. They are the guardians of the Brisingamen necklace, but little else is known about them.

Dragon: Dragons were about the size of an elephant and were found in Europe, the Middle East, Asia Minor, India and South-east Asia. According to legend, they lived in caves in mountainous areas and could easily live for 400 years.

The Grey Man: Made of nothing but mist, this imaginary person comes from Irish folk tales. His origins remain mysterious.

Griffon: This creature occurs in the mythologies of India, the Near East and western Russia. Part eagle and part lion, the griffon was the emblem of powerful emperors and great rulers of several realms. They are said to live for fifty or sixty years and inhabit mountains.

Kelpie: In Gaelic, Kelpies are known as 'each uisge' or 'tarbh uisge' meaning 'water bulls'. They live in lakes and rivers, are the size of a horse and form part of Scottish and Irish mythology.

Leprechaun: An ancient Irish name for imps who love playing tricks. They are believed to hide pots of gold at the end of the rainbow and are as much a symbol of Ireland as the four-leaf clover.

Mermen: In Ireland the sea dwellers are known as 'mermen'. They can be distinguished from other aquatic creatures by their red bonnets with feathers. This magic headgear helps them descend to their home in the ocean depths. The females are very beautiful and the sight of them is supposed to indicate a coming storm. Mermen can sometimes appear on land.

Seahorse: The giant seahorse is found in legends in the Mediterranean, the Red Sea and the Indian Ocean. In the Sinbad stories these creatures live in warm waters, scouring the seas in packs.

Sea Serpent: These serpents live in all seas and oceans throughout the world. According to explorers' tales, they can reach lengths of over sixty metres. Some crypto-zoologists think that they may be plesiosaurs (marine lizards or reptiles) that survived from the era of the dinosaurs.

Siren: The origins of these sea creatures remain obscure. They have appeared in the myths and legends of many cultures since ancient times. They are usually beautiful women with fishes' tails who cast their spell on fishermen so that their boats will be dashed on the rocks.

Witch: Witches are found in the mythology of nearly all cultures. They are generally terribly ugly and often attack children. In this book Baba Yaga is drawn from Baba Gaya, an ogress appearing in Russian fairy tales who flies about in her cauldron to capture and eat small children.

AMOS DARAGON

BOOK FIVE

THE TOWER OF EL-BAB

BRYAN PERRO

Scribo

A division of Book House

PROLOGUE

AMOS DARAGON
THE TOWER OF EL-BAB

T he ancient legends of the Norsemen tell of the necklace of Brisingamen. It was made by Alfrigg, Dvalin, Berling and Grer, four burly, long-bearded dwarves, and was once one of the wonders of the world. According to the legend, Freyja, goddess of Love and Fertility, wanted to possess the necklace in order to enhance her already impressive beauty. To achieve her desire, she put a spell on the dwarves and cheated them by spiriting away Brisingamen. The story relates that when she returned to Åsgard, the home of the gods, her great beauty lit it up like a new sun. Odin, the chief of the Nordic gods, ordered her to return the necklace to its rightful owners. The dwarves had appealed to him and demanded restitution. They wanted their property returned.

Odin declared that this theft had brought shame on the gods of Good and was unworthy of such a beautiful and noble soul as Freyja. The goddess refused to submit to Odin's will and gave the necklace into the keeping of the Brising, a race of fairies that dwelt in the depths of the snow-covered forests. So it was that neither Odin nor the dwarves could lay hands on it.

Because of this necklace, war broke out between Freyja's armies and those of Odin. The conflict lasted for several decades and brought about the death of hundreds of Vikings and the extinction of many magical creatures. Everyone knew the bear-men were Odin's favourite creatures. In order to have her revenge, Freyja placed a curse on the Beorites so that their infants died in the cradle, thus condemning their race to certain extinction.

The ancient sages knew well that when the gods of Good quarrel among themselves, the gods of Evil take their chance to extend their power over the Earth. Thus it has been since the beginning of time.

BOOK HOUSE

DRAGONS

- Paperback   £4.99
- 282 x 219 mm; 48pp
- Interest 7+
- Full-colour artwork
- Glossary, contents and index

ISBN: 9781905638291

caly creatures spewing fire? Terrible beasts spreading clouds of poison? The special emblems of Chinese emperors? Find out the fantastic truth about dragons, the creatures who, from the beginning of time, have haunted the imagination and dreams of almost every culture in the world.

VISIT THE AMOS DARAGON WEBSITE:
www.amosdaragon.co.uk
OR VISIT BOOK HOUSE AT:
www.book-house.co.uk